Becca began

Kody,

Met Miss Becca. Quite a catch…if this woman really *is* going to marry you. I'll be back tomorrow at 10:00 a.m. for proof. Otherwise, I'll start proceedings to sell. Remember the terms: no wife, no heir, no ranch.

——Mr. Griswold, Attorney-at-law

Heart pounding, Becca read the message again. With every sentence, the fragile hopes she'd clung to splintered and fell away.

Kody had just been using her to fulfill the terms of his father's will!

Dear Reader,

In Arlene James's *Desperately Seeking Daddy*, a harried, single working mom of three feels like Cinderella at the ball when Jack Tyler comes into her life. He wins over her kids, charms her mother and sets straight her grumpy boss. He's the FABULOUS FATHER of her kids' dreams—and the husband of hers!

Although the BUNDLE OF JOY in Amelia Varden's arms is not her natural child, she's loved the baby boy from birth. And now one man has come to claim her son—and her heart—in reader favorite Elizabeth August's *The Rancher and the Baby*.

Won't You Be My Husband? begins Linda Varner's trilogy HOME FOR THE HOLIDAYS, in which a woman ends up engaged to be married after a ten-minute reunion with a bad-boy hunk!

What's a smitten bookkeeper to do when her gorgeous boss asks her to be his bride—even for convenience? Run down the aisle!…in DeAnna Talcott's *The Bachelor and the Bassinet*.

In Pat Montana's *Storybook Bride*, tight-lipped rancher Kody Sanville's been called a half-breed his whole life and doesn't believe in storybook anything. So why can't he stop dreaming of being loved by Becca Covington?

Suzanne McMinn makes her **debut** with *Make Room for Mommy*, in which a single woman with motherhood and marriage on her mind falls for a single dad who isn't at all interested in saying "I do"…or so he thinks!

From classic love stories, to romantic comedies to emotional heart tuggers, Silhouette Romance offers six wonderful new novels each month by six talented authors. I hope you enjoy all six books this month—and every month.

Regards,

Melissa Senate,
Senior Editor

Please address questions and book requests to:
Silhouette Reader Service
U.S.: 3010 Walden Ave., P.O. Box 1325, Buffalo, NY 14269
Canadian: P.O. Box 609, Fort Erie, Ont. L2A 5X3

STORYBOOK BRIDE

Pat Montana

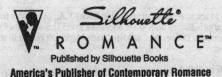

Silhouette®

ROMANCE™

Published by Silhouette Books

America's Publisher of Contemporary Romance

To my sister, Judy,
supporter and friend.

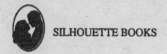

SILHOUETTE BOOKS

ISBN 0-373-19190-1

STORYBOOK BRIDE

Printed in U.S.A.

Books by Pat Montana

Silhouette Romance

One Unbelievable Man #993
Babies Inc. #1076
Storybook Cowboy #1111
Storybook Bride #1190

PAT MONTANA

grew up in Colorado, but now lives in the Midwest. So far she's been a wife, mother of four adopted daughters and a grandmother. She's also been a soda jerk, secretary, teacher, counselor, artist—and an author. She considers life an adventure and plans to live to be at least one hundred because she has so many things to do.

Some of the goals Pat has set for herself include being a volunteer rocker for disadvantaged babies and teaching in the literacy program. She wants to learn to weave and to throw pots on a wheel, not to mention learn French, see a play at the Parthenon in Greece and sing in a quartet. Above all, she wants to write more romances.

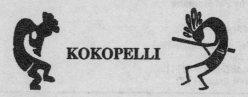

KOKOPELLI

The Hopi Kachina, called Kokopelli or the Humpbacked Flute player, was a favorite subject of prehistoric artists of the Southwest, seemingly then—as now—associated with fertility.

In many Native American tribes, the flute was used only for one kind of music—love and courting music. Its melodies were believed to have such power, to make a man so irresistible, that any woman who heard them would follow the sound and surrender herself to the player.

So what do you think is bound to happen when our heroine, Becca Covington, hears the music of a flute one evening? Turn the pages of *Storybook Bride* to find out....

Chapter One

The Covington ranch was the perfect setting for a wedding.

Becca Covington stole around the side of the bride's tent for one last, calm look before she got caught up in the whirl of music and flowers and smiling faces. She had to prepare herself for the ordeal of getting down the white canvas aisle without reacting to Kody Sanville.

With an impatient flick of her hand, she shushed a bee circling her carefully curled hair and tried to focus on the meadow filled with summer wildflowers and brightly dressed guests. Why, there must be more than a hundred people out there. Most of the white chairs were already filled. Who would have thought so many friends and family would come all the way to New Mexico for a wedding? Especially a wedding on a ranch in the middle of nowhere.

Ah, but these were the Covingtons, Becca reminded herself. Covington ceremonies were *social events,* and

Covington rites were always perfect, if they had to pay for them themselves to guarantee it. This one would be no exception, she knew—a perfect wedding...on a perfectly lovely day...in a spot that was perfectly unique.

Thank goodness the wedding wasn't hers.

Shrugging off a twinge of guilt, she turned to rejoin her brother's bride-to-be and the other bridesmaids inside the white tent.

"You know what a bind I'm in. I need your help."

Kody Sanville. Becca's pulse kicked up at the sound of his deep voice. Darn. Only two days since they'd met at the rehearsal, and she already recognized his voice. He'd hardly spoken to her since, yet his few words had wreaked havoc with her breathing.

It was the altitude, that was all. Oxygen deprivation. New Mexico was a lot higher than Vermont. Raising her hand to quiet the flutter in her chest, she moved back to the tent.

"I'm sorry, Kody."

A woman's voice. Callie Keams? Becca's flutter took on a host of new dimensions—sympathy for the attractive woman from the nearby pueblo who was paired with Kody in the wedding party, admiration for her courage. And a needling touch of...jealousy?

"I want to help, Kody, but this is more than I can..." Callie's voice faded.

No. Jealousy was absurd. Callie seemed to be standing up to Kody, which was more than Becca ever intended to do. They'd have to *pay* her to confront Kody. His eyes were much too dark and stern. Too disapproving.

She reached for the tent flap, careful to keep her satin dress from rustling. Eavesdropping was not what she'd come out here for, especially not on Kody. He already made her nervous, and she sure didn't want him catching her in a compromising situation.

"I don't want the job, Kody."

The tent flap slipped from Becca's hand. *Job?* One little three-letter word—was that all it took to make her suddenly ignore her scruples?

"What about the ranch? And The Journey?"

"I can't help you this time, Kody. Not...like this. No, please don't ask again. I think you must ask Kokopelli."

The sound of hurried footsteps shocked Becca into motion, but before she could slip inside the tent, Callie rushed by. Becca barely caught a glimpse of her unhappy face and the dark braid down the back of her turquoise dress.

Peering around the corner of the tent, Becca searched for Kody. He looked even more disturbed as he stalked away in the opposite direction.

"Mr. Sanville!" Lord, had she lost her mind? Had she actually called his name?

She struggled for balance in her high heels, stepping cautiously across the uneven ground. Five minutes before her brother's wedding was definitely not the time to break an ankle. "Kody, wait!"

He turned, and she forgot all about walking carefully... or about walking at all.

He was wearing a tuxedo. She couldn't believe what that did to her breathing. He looked like a magnificent giant, like a wild mustang done up in the trappings of a parade horse. He'd pulled his thick, shoulder-length hair behind his ears—black satin brushing the ebony of his jacket collar. His white pleated shirt shone like snow next to the bronze of his skin, and a white rosebud adorned his lapel like a delicate blossom on a dark, majestic tree.

All she could think was that he looked devastating. All she could feel was her pulse threatening a complete runaway.

She'd never seen him without his hat. In the bright sunlight, she could see the breadth of his bronze forehead and the deep V between his black eyebrows, as if a frown had taken up permanent residence there. Lines radiated from the corners of his dark eyes and bracketed his mouth like etchings. Evidence of hard knocks—too many for a man her brother said was barely in his thirties.

Without his hat, Kody looked uncomfortable, as if she'd caught him half-undressed. Without his hat, he looked...vulnerable.

But he still wore his boots. She forced herself to focus on them while she struggled to regain her composure. Not even a wedding could make Kody give up the black, ornately tooled footwear. He'd planted those boots firmly apart on the uneven ground, as if to assure himself of firm footing.

He looked solid as a rock...which was a lot more than she could claim at the moment. Her heartbeat didn't slow when she saw the V deepen between his brows.

"Wedding starts in five minutes."

His words rumbled like distant thunder, but she couldn't let that stop her. She'd made it past prairie dog holes and rocks...probably a couple of snakes...but what lay ahead loomed a whole lot more threatening.

"I couldn't help overhearing your conversation... with Callie?"

His hard gaze triggered a rush of panic, sent her hands searching for pockets, then curling into the satin folds of her skirt.

"Listen, I've backpacked and camped out. And I've won ribbons for riding." She was still having trouble breathing; it *had* to be the altitude. She never let a man intimidate her.

Kody barely lifted one dark brow, but she didn't think it was because he was impressed.

"What I mean is, I'll take that job Callie turned down."

That brought a distinct snort.

She ought to pay attention. Just what did she think she was doing, anyhow? As soon as Trey's wedding was over, she was going back home to look for a job at one of the social service agencies in Montpelier. Now that she'd gotten her degree, she wanted a position that would let her work full-time with disadvantaged children.

So why was she pressing for a job here? On a ranch? With cows? And possibly the grouchiest Native American in all of New Mexico?

Because she was crazy, that was why. Suffering from altitude sickness.

"Look, I'm not...going back to Vermont right away." The minute she said it, she knew it was true. She needed to be away from her father and brothers for a while. Away from Allen. If her brothers wrote her one more résumé, if they lined up one more job interview with some nice old lady at some quaint private charity, she would probably disown them. If her fiancé warned her again that the kids she wanted to help would only break her heart, if he asked her *one more time* to move in with him, she would—

"Go to work here, on your brother's ranch." Kody's frown deepened but he didn't move to leave.

"He has all the help he needs." And she didn't want her family doing her any more favors. She loved the men in her life, but they tried to protect her too much. Especially since Mom died.

Her fingers found the charm hanging from the chain around her neck, the twisted knot of gold that had been her mother's. If Becca was going to help kids, she had to know she could take care of herself, that she wasn't dependent like her mother had always been.

Kody Sanville would be the kind of boss who'd insist she take care of herself.

"Look, you don't have to interview that 'Coco Pelly' person. I'll report for work as soon as the wedding is over."

For the first time since they'd met, Becca could feel Kody really looking at her. His brows rose in amazement and his gaze dropped to her shoes, starting a slow ascent that made her wince with every rejecting pause: *sheer* nylons, *pink* dress, *less-than-modest* neckline, *bare* shoulders. Big diamond ring. She felt as if she were being tried and found guilty—of utter frivolousness.

He stopped at her hair and actually squinted. She could almost read his final dismissal—*curly-headed blond bimbo.* Clearly he was sentencing her to hanging. Or maybe a scalping.

Oh dear. She smothered a panicked laugh. Only her brothers would appreciate that kind of dark humor. But to her amazement, a flicker of amusement turned one corner of Kody's mouth.

Had he read her mind? Could there possibly be humor buried under all that dark reserve? She tried a tentative smile.

Kody just turned on his booted heel and strode away.

"Hey! Wait a minute. *Kody—*?"

"Forget it, Miss Covington." He glanced back over his shoulder, and there was no sign of amusement in his face. "You probably don't know a skunk from a house cat. The job isn't open. Not to a soft city woman."

Soft. Kody swallowed an oath, sharp and blunt, one of the white man's words he'd learned from his father. It stuck in his chest, lodged like a spiny cactus pad. How did he expect to scare Rebecca Covington off if words like *soft* kept forcing themselves into his awareness?

A scent, sweet and delicate, pursued him as he tramped away from her. Deliberately, he blew out a puff of air, followed by a terse Hopi word he'd picked up during his short childhood with his mother. That didn't help, either.

Just outside the entrance to the groom's tent he stopped, tugged at the tight black bow tie, wiped a boot on the back of a pant leg . . . and caught himself looking for her.

He watched her pick her way across to the bride's tent set up at the back of the rows of seats. It was a wonder she hadn't broken her damned, stocking-clad, pretty little ankle the way she'd barreled after him across the uneven meadowland.

But he knew he was just blowing off steam with such churlish thoughts. Even in those impossible pink shoes, Becca Covington moved with a grace and surefootedness that unsettled him. And watching her blond hair sway like prairie grass curling in a breeze did little to restore his usual stoicism. Or help him think clearly about how to deal with his dilemma.

Because Callie's turndown had left him with a full-fledged dilemma. *'Bout like tryin' to find a horse thief in heaven,* J.S. would say. Becca looked as if she'd flown in first-class from heaven, but nothing on earth would convince him to hire her. Especially not as his wife.

No wife, no heir, no ranch, his father's smarmy attorney had told him the will said. But he'd be damned if he'd involve Rebecca Covington in his problems. Yanking down his black satin cummerbund, he shoved into the tent, the words echoing like a curse.

"Hey, Kody." Trey Covington looked up from the card table where he was collecting playing cards from his brothers. "I'm quitting even though I'm winning. My intentions are truly honorable, even if you didn't think so at first."

"You aren't at the altar yet, old bro." Andy, the youngest, punched Trey's shoulder. Ted, the serious one, stood and checked his watch.

Trey slid an arm into his tuxedo jacket. "Who you calling old, little brother? Try mature. Or seasoned."

"How 'bout *ready?* The processional just started."

"Guess this is it, huh, guys?" Trey wrestled with his black bow tie. "Thanks for being here."

The minister appeared at the tent opening, and Ted and Andy followed him outside.

With the brothers gone, Kody turned to Trey. "You are an honorable man, *Sikyahonaw.*" He called Trey Yellow Bear, from the language of his mother's people. He'd never learned the word for *brother...* and long ago forgotten the word for *friend.* Though he'd spent most of his life resenting the *bahana*—the white man of his father's world—Trey had truly become like a brother to Kody.

Although when Kody had first met Trey, he'd distrusted this "cowboy" from Vermont. But Trey had won the love of Kody's good friend, Jo McPherson. Now

Trey and Jo would be fulfilling Trey's crazy dream, The Covington Camel Ranch, together.

"I wish you harmony in your marriage with Jo. And much happiness." Kody offered his hand, and was startled when Trey pulled him into a hug.

"Thanks, Kody. Thanks, brother."

Kody stepped back, straightened his shoulders and cleared his throat, but Trey was already on the move. Following him outside, Kody stretched to his full height and took his place between Andy and Trey, facing the rows of seated guests.

He was proud to be one of Trey's groomsmen, but he knew there was no place in the Covington family for another brother. Not one with skin the color of adobe.

Firmly he pushed the thought aside. This wasn't the time to nurse old wounds, not when his friend was about to be married. Not when beautiful music hummed through the crystalline air. Only a wealthy family like the Covingtons would hire a string quartet for a ranch wedding. Near the front, he saw Trey's third brother, Mitch, playing with the group.

The volume of the music rose, and Kody's gaze shifted to the back. Right on cue, Billy, Trey's six-year-old son from his failed first marriage, began the long trek up the white canvas of the center aisle.

Kody couldn't help smiling. Billy's suit and cowboy boots matched Trey's exactly, just like the shock of sun-bleached hair that fell across his forehead. And he looked as if his very life depended on getting the white ring cushion to the front.

He would probably catch a raft of teasing about that later. Kidding and heckling seemed to be the basic form of communication among the Covington offspring. Yet

Kody knew the bond between them was strong. A blood bond.

An ache stirred somewhere in his chest, like healed bones that still protested before rain. The Covington bonds weren't like the Sanville bonds. The only ties he'd known had been broken by the time he was six.

The sight of the matron of honor taking her place at the front pulled him from his brooding, but he fought the need to look back down the aisle. He knew who was coming next. He'd already seen too much of Becca today.

Before she had arrived, Trey had told Kody that Becca was the only one in the Covington family like him. What he hadn't said was that she was as fair and warm as sunlight. Or that her eyes laughed whenever she spoke. He hadn't said her voice was like the soft roughness of suede.

Brothers didn't say things like that, Kody supposed. Maybe they didn't even know.

But Kody knew. And he had no right to think such things about Rebecca Covington. She was *bahana*. She wore an engagement ring. But he couldn't stop himself from watching her glide up the aisle in her dress the color of sunrise, her soft hair spilling around her shoulders like liquid gold. She was as fresh and bright as a spring morning and as full of light. When her silver-green gaze found his, he felt again the pounding of his heart.

The sound turned to thunder when he saw the flash of conviction in her eyes. Another time he might have cursed, but the word slipped away. This soft city woman thought she could work on his ranch with only back-packing and camping experience? She probably even rode an English saddle! He might as well hire a Girl Scout.

If he hired Becca, J.S. would laugh him right out of the kitchen. *She'd be about as much good at the ranch as a hen at a mass meeting of coyotes,* J.S. would declare. And he'd be right. If there were two things J.S. knew, they were ranch cooking and ranch hands. Becca Covington was definitely not ranch-hand material.

Kody wished he'd never laid eyes on her. He'd be damned if he'd let her stir the Sanville passions.

With sheer force of will, he turned his attention to the last bridesmaid. Callie was a different kind of beauty, a woman a man could find comfort in—with dark eyes set wide above wider cheekbones, skin a warm earthen color, a thick black braid, a dress the color of "sky in the stone."

He'd heard Mitch call her *exotic.* Strange word for a woman who to him seemed more like an earth mother. Callie accepted Kody for what he was.

As she neared, she smiled and held his gaze, and he suffered a wash of guilt. He'd been wrong to trade on her friendship, wrong to ask her to pretend to be the wife he would never ask her to become.

Stepping forward, he offered his arm, led her to the altar of flowers in front and separated from her to take his place at the end of the line of groomsmen. From there he watched the guests rise as the traditional music announced the entry of the bride.

As white as a summer cloud, Jo McPherson floated up the aisle on the arm of her elderly father to take her place beside Trey. She gazed up at him lovingly.

Jo would stay beside Trey forever, Kody knew. The *bahana* rings promised that, like the promise of the Hopi wedding gift—the pair of white moccasins for the bride. He knew just as well that he would never give such a gift. He would not repeat the sins of his father.

His attorney would just have to figure out how to break the terms of his father's will. Just as Kody had figured out how to change the Sanville $ brand into the Sanville Star.

Kody forced his gaze back from where it had strayed to Becca. He wanted the Sanville Star Ranch more than anything he'd wanted in his life.

But he would never marry to get it.

"Kody!"

Kody pretended not to hear the whisper as he stood with the wedding party in the reception line under the party canopy. Instead, he smiled and shook the hand of a white-haired lady working her way down the line. It didn't take a Harvard graduate to know Becca was trying to get his attention. She still radiated the same delicate fragrance she carried wherever she went.

"Kody? *Ko*-dy!"

A tug on his sleeve made him glance behind Andy, who was standing next to him.

"I need to talk to you," she whispered, peering around Andy's back. She didn't look the least bit ruffled at being caught about to tug his sleeve again.

Andy leaned toward Kody. "I'd suggest you talk to her, man. I've never known her to give up."

Desperately Kody searched the crowd. Where was Callie when he needed her? Probably huddled somewhere with her cellular phone. Those contraptions should be illegal on a ranch.

Andy shook the gloved hand of the last woman and passed her along to Kody with a wide grin. "I'm outta here," he whispered. "Good luck with my lovely but persistent sister. Now, where's the champagne?"

Like ice on a hot griddle, the entire reception line seemed to melt away, following Andy in the direction of refreshments. Except for Becca. As quickly as Andy strode off, she stepped into the space next to Kody.

"Kody, I want to talk to you about that job."

Her textured voice raised the hair on the back of his neck. He couldn't very well pretend he hadn't heard her. Bracing himself, he turned and was startled again by how small she was. Even in those ridiculous heels, she had to turn her face up to talk to him. A man would have to lean clear over if he wanted to—

"The job isn't open." He bit the words off to interrupt what he'd been contemplating, but his growl didn't seem to affect her. Becca just smiled, showing off faint dimples.

That unsettled him more. What she needed was the Sanville scowl, the glare that had run off more preppie white boys than he cared to remember.

Becca didn't even blink, but the dimple hovered in her cheek, threatening to undo another layer of his resolve.

"Look, Becca, I don't need—"

"Kody?"

Relief swept through him at the sound of Callie's voice. In spite of the uneven terrain, she hurried toward them from the direction of the caterer's truck.

"Kody, it's J.S. He's in the hospital in Santa Fe."

"Hospital?" Becca stepped forward. "Nothing serious, I hope."

"I'm afraid it might be," Callie answered. "J.S. had a heart attack and is in intensive care. If he holds his own through the night, they'll do some tests to decide about surgery. Possibly tomorrow."

"Bypass surgery?" Kody started to walk away, not waiting for the shock to settle in. J.S. was the closest thing to a father he'd ever known. "I've got to see him." But hard-earned white man's manners brought him to a stop.

"Becca?" He reached for the hat that always rode low on his brow, but his thumb nudged empty air. Damn. "J.S. is more than just my cook. He's . . . a friend. Will you explain to Trey and Jo?"

"Of course. Go right now. They'll understand."

"Wait, Kody." Callie put her hand on his arm. "The doctor said . . . only family. Until after the tests."

Only family. The words hit him like a punch in the gut.

"J.S. sent you a message. Said to tell you to quit worrying like a duck in the desert and get busy finding yourself another cook."

Kody let out a controlled breath and forced himself to stay calm. "Guess if he had enough wind to get all that out, he's not ready for the happy hunting ground."

Callie offered a worried half smile, but her understanding didn't help Kody. He cared as much about Callie's grandfather as she did, but the truth was, Kody wasn't family. He had no family. Never would.

"I'll let you know how he's doing."

Before he could stop her, Callie slipped away, leaving him alone with Becca.

Suddenly the tuxedo felt too restricting. He shoved his fists into the trouser pockets to keep from checking his watch, knowing that any time was too much before he could get out of these *bahana* clothes and back to the ranch. Back to where he belonged. But he couldn't just run off.

"Maybe we should join the others." He headed toward the party canopies, much too aware of Becca beside him. Too conscious of the concern on her face.

"I'm sorry about your friend."

"Yeah." He didn't want her sympathy.

"Things'll probably be pretty tough at the ranch without him."

"We'll manage." He didn't need Becca's understanding, either. What he needed was a cook who could stir up a mess of chili and a pot of boiled coffee, a ranch hand who could drive a team of mules and manage a herd of predelinquent boys.

And a woman who would act the starry-eyed fiancée whenever his father's attorney showed up. He might as well ask for the moon.

"Kody, I know this might not be a good time for it, but the thing is . . . I can cook."

That brought him to an abrupt stop. Given a hundred yards—or a hundred years—he might convince himself that Becca was no more than a confection, a cloud of pink cotton candy at the local rodeo. But up close like this, in that dress that showed too damn much of her glowing skin, she was about as easy to ignore as a bright cactus flower.

But he would ignore her. "I don't need any Vermont cream puff of a debutante in my kitchen."

Too late to call the words back—he saw her dusty green eyes widen, couldn't stop watching the faint pink that started in her cheeks and slipped down her slender neck to color her bare shoulders. Damn.

"Cooking for ranch hands is different," he managed to grunt out.

She tilted her head, and he saw that flash of determination again. "I doubt it's much different from cooking for a father and four picky brothers. Besides, I learn fast." Her eyes narrowed noticeably. "And just for the record, Kody, I was never a debutante."

He'd bet she'd never cooked up beans and sowbelly in a cast-iron pot, either, or stopped a fight between boys whose anger was too big for their britches. He bet she'd never wanted for anything in her life.

Not the way he wanted this ranch.

Suddenly he knew there were times in a man's life when he had to act, when the ends had to justify the means.

Maybe, under all that prettiness, Becca was like her brother Trey—someone Kody could depend on. Maybe she could give him the few weeks he needed—just until J.S. got back on his feet.

"Okay, Becca, you got yourself a job."

Now all Kody had to do was keep his distance.

Chapter Two

The Sanville Star Ranch didn't look like it would exactly require survival skills to endure. Becca stared up at the massive two-story ranch house set off by mountains in the distance and thought of the forts her brothers had once built of toy logs. Yet, the only thing fortlike about this house were the huge logs. Everything else spoke of money.

A fancy spindled rocking chair sat on the covered porch, and above, the windows fluttered with lace curtains. The wood that framed the entrance was painted a beautiful blue, and carved birds decorated the wooden screen door.

Becca's heart sank like a slowly deflating balloon. This felt more like checking into Club Med than reporting for a crash course in self-reliance. All indications suggested she'd made the worst decision of her life.

Whirling, she searched for the Jeep Andy had brought her in before he joined the rest of the family to return to

Vermont. But it sped away, disappearing in a cloud of dust down the long, juniper-lined road to the highway.

Too late to stop him. Becca sighed. Probably just as well. After arguing a whole day with her brothers, she couldn't back out now or they'd never let her live it down. Trey had been the only one to support her decision.

And her fiancé had been worse than her brothers! She picked up her suitcase and backpack and turned to the ranch house, trying to forget Allen's words when she'd called him last night. *You should get an employment contract so the man can't work you too hard.* He'd even offered to call Kody and negotiate for her!

Renewed anger set her in motion. She'd show Allen and her brothers she could cope. She didn't need them protecting her from the realities of life anymore. No more shielding her like they had her mother. Hefting the bags higher, she marched toward the wide porch stairs.

"Afternoon, Becca."

The sound of Kody's deep voice stopped her on the first step. He stood just inside the door, his silhouette filling the doorway, his hat scant inches from the lintel. He looked like a shadow of a bear until he swung the screen door open and stepped out.

She clutched the bags tighter, glad they kept her hand from flying to the gold charm at her throat...where her heart seemed to have lodged.

"Reporting for work," she managed to croak with about three times more conviction than she felt. He looked as grim as a TV lawyer and not a bit happy to see her. The luggage slipped in her hands from the dampness gathering there.

"You're right on time."

The unexpected approval in his voice caught her off guard, but she couldn't find evidence of it in his face. The sooner she got away from him and started to work, the sooner she'd be able to breathe normally again.

"Which way to the bunkhouse?"

"I'll show you the main house first." Eyes hidden in the shade of his hat, Kody glided soundlessly down the stairs and across the dusty ground. Without looking at her, he lifted the suitcase and backpack from her hands.

She tried to protest, but the shock of his gentle touch left her without air. She drew in a halting breath laced with his earthy, masculine scent. Intoxicating. It drew her after him.

"Wait." She followed him up the stairs. "Kody, I know you have cows to round up and fences to fix...."

He disappeared through the wide doorway, leaving the carved screen door standing open.

"And you don't need to do things for me." Stepping inside, she closed the screen behind her. "I can carry my own things, and I can find my way arou—" She came to a stop. "This is a *ranch* house?"

A broad staircase with curving banisters of light wood rose from the center of the entryway, and Oriental rugs decorated the deep red terra-cotta tiles of the floor. The walls on either side were stuccoed in rich adobe and adorned with colorful paintings.

She'd heard of gentlemen farmers, but for a man who raised cows, this seemed a mighty fancy place to hang his hat.

"Kody, this is...lovely."

But clearly not designed for a range-worn cowhand. It didn't even look as if Kody lived here. He had too many rough edges, too much restlessness for a house like this.

"My father wanted to attract the 'right' people," he muttered. "To run his cattle business. Never lived here himself. He died three months ago. That's when I moved in." He set the backpack and suitcase next to the stairs. Snatching off his white straw hat, he paced to the back wall and hung it on a peg.

"I'm sorry about your father," Becca murmured.

Kody didn't answer.

Becca crossed her arms and wished her heart would settle. Kody's blunt words explained why he seemed so uncomfortable inside the elegant ranch house. She could sympathize with his loss, but looking at him didn't help her pulse slow. His hair was drawn back into a ponytail, setting off the rugged planes of his face. His faded denim shirt and worn jeans molded the contours of his solid body like a glove.

She struggled for a breath. She'd never studied a man like this. Not even Allen.

Kody strode to the archway on the left. "You'll have the run of the house, of course, just like the other hands. Except for my quarters. They're . . . off the kitchen."

He paused under the archway, his face creased in the already familiar frown. He didn't seem too happy that his room was next to where she'd be cooking.

She managed to squelch the teasing she would have shot back at her brothers. The thought that surfaced instead made her temperature rise. Wondering what Kody's bedroom looked like didn't exactly qualify as innocent curiosity.

"Front room," he murmured, dismissing everything in the open space with one sweep of his large hand. "The men come in to watch TV sometimes."

The big-screen TV was impressive, but it was the huge stone fireplace across the end wall that captured her attention...along with the leather sofas the color of deerskin and the dappled hide on the hardwood floor. A place where a cowboy could settle in, soak up the warmth of a roaring fire...and have his feet rubbed.

She tried to imagine Kody there, but the picture wouldn't take shape. Quickly she turned away, lifting her hat and ponytail to cool the back of her neck. "I hope the kitchen is as marvelous as the rest."

"First you have to get moved in." He strode back to the entryway, where he started up the stairs with her bags.

Alarm hit fast. "Wait a minute! I thought I'd be staying in the bunkhouse." The last thing she wanted was a room in the house where Kody slept. *Lived,* she corrected herself hastily. "Look, Kody, why don't I just stay where your cook does. With the rest of the hands."

Almost imperceptibly, his dark brows rose. "You ready to share with the men? No separate rooms. One big open shower. No doors in the john."

If she had to stay in the ranch house, there'd be *no independence.* She didn't need another man checking on her comings and goings. She didn't want to be aware of Kody's.

But he wasn't offering much choice. "I guess you'll have to show me the room upstairs."

He started up again, but not before she saw the amusement in his eyes.

So there *was* humor under all that impossible reserve. But, darn it, he was laughing at her...just like her brothers. Except that laughter in Kody's eyes wasn't annoying. It was unnerving.

Reluctantly, she followed him up the stairs. At the top, he opened a door on the right and stepped back, nodding for her to enter.

The room wasn't large, but the bed was—a full king-size with a beautiful curved headboard of white wrought iron above a star-patterned quilt of aqua, peach and mauve. The sight of it made her face warm again.

She hurried in, keeping her back toward him. "What a beautiful room." It looked as if it had been decorated for a woman untouched by ranching life. Lace curtains fluttering at the windows, puffy pillows overflowing a rocking chair, braided rugs scattered across the floor—the room was feminine and inviting. But the bed was much too large. Becca ran nervous fingers along the marble-topped dresser. Its coolness brought her to her senses. "This is a wonderful room, Kody, but I don't want to put someone out."

"It's never been used. The rancher who ran the place for my father didn't have a family. Most of the rooms upstairs were closed off."

Some decorator had created a beautiful illusion in this room, but everything looked untouched. No one had ever loved this room, or loved *in* it. The thought brought her gaze unwillingly back to Kody.

He still stood outside the door. "Bath's over there, extra towels and sheets in the chest. Closet's empty. Luce Garcia will come in to clean and wash on Fridays. She'll take care of everything for you."

It occurred to her then that he was feeling as uncomfortable as she was. Though she wanted to protest being taken care of, another part of her warmed at his discomfort.

"Do I have to pay ransom for my suitcases?" She couldn't stop a smile from creeping into her eyes, couldn't resist the impulse to tease him as he stood so cautiously outside what was to be her bedroom.

Ducking his head, he carried her luggage in and bounced them onto the bed, then backed once more to the doorway.

She could tell he was coming to the end of his tolerance. For being trapped indoors? For spending time with her? She wasn't sure which, but she was just as anxious for him to be gone as he was.

This wasn't turning out as she'd hoped. Instead of learning self-reliance, she'd be indulged with a pretty room in a fancy ranch house—with a cleaning lady to pick up after her! Instead of becoming an independent ranch hand, she'd be cooking right next to her boss's sleeping quarters. A boss who squirmed at mixing business and bedrooms.

Worst of all, she found that rather... tantalizing.

Quickly she crossed to the bed and busied herself opening her suitcase.

"Thanks for showing me around. I'll get unpacked and check out the kitchen. I don't think I'll have any trouble, but if I have any questions, I'll just ask whoever's around."

"No."

Kody barely stepped back into the room, but his concern seemed to fill it.

"No?" She watched his dark eyes grow even darker.

"I don't want the other men distracted from their work. If you have questions, ask *me*. You can unpack later. I'll show you the kitchen now." He turned on his heel and disappeared through the doorway.

He might as well have thrown her into the horse-watering tank. She stared after him, struggling with disappointment and anger. Anger won.

He wanted her to ask *him*? Right. When his cows took off flying! Besides, what would she ask, except what she was supposed to do between meals? Or more to the point, what she *wasn't* supposed to do, since he seemed to be laying the rules down so fast.

What had become of making her own decisions? Of coping with things on her own? Working for Kody Sanville sounded as if it would be worse than dealing with her brothers, father and fiancé all rolled together.

"*Ex*-fiancé, if he's not careful," she grumbled, slapping her hat down onto the bed. Allen's attitude about taking this job was what had finally made her postpone their wedding. And whatever Kody's problem was, *his* attitude was exactly what she needed to get her priorities back in order.

The sooner he showed her the kitchen and told her the rest of his silly rules, the sooner he'd go away. Then she could start working on taking care of herself.

Hiring Becca Covington to work at the ranch was just plain dumb, Kody decided, watching her trot down the wide staircase. He tried not to breathe in her light, airy scent, perfume that whispered of femininity... and *bahana* background.

If J.S. knew about Becca, he'd be lying in his hospital bed laughing his head off. *You got nothin' under your hat but hair, man?* he'd say. *You must be plumb weak north of the ears if you think you can move that little filly in and pretend she's not there. Why, she's as soft an' fluffy as a goose-hair pillow.*

Soft. There was that damnable word again. Designer-label jeans and a denim shirt with ruffles on it didn't do much better than that sugarplum bridesmaid dress to hide her supple body—*or* her inexperience with ranch life.

Soft city woman. Hair like sunshine and silk. She didn't belong here.

But she looked as if she did. The realization hit him hard. Becca was the kind of woman his father had created the house for, not for the son whose family, on his mother's side, wore moccasins.

A well-used curse flew to his tongue, but he quashed it into silence. His father might have thought he could control his son's life from the grave, but Kody would find a way to break that will.

As for Becca, he had only himself to blame for her being here. Once he showed her the kitchen and spelled out her job, he'd stay away from her. Eat in the barn if he had to.

Pacing to the back of the entryway, he retrieved his hat and clapped it securely back onto his head.

Becca moved through the archway to the dining room and began to circle, touching the country cupboard on the long wall and the carved *trastero* cupboard at the end, almost as if she were greeting them.

The gesture touched the hollow place in his chest.

She stopped at the table. "This looks more like real *ranch* furniture."

"Bought it at an auction. Stuff in here before wouldn't have survived a week." He watched her trace slender, manicured fingers along the scarred oak table and felt hen flesh rise across his shoulders. She wasn't wearing the big diamond ring anymore.

"You could feed the whole Covington clan right here." Her gaze flew to him. "How many *will* I be cooking for?"

Kody resisted the urge to scrub at the back of his neck. "Five, counting yourself. Next week we start summer grazing. There'll be five more then."

Tugging his hat low, he avoided her eyes. He should tell her there would be five *boys*—five misfits like the kind of kid he'd been, with no place to call a real home. Kids who were already courting trouble with the law. He should tell her about The Journey, his program for delinquent youths.

That wasn't the only thing he should tell her.

If she knew he was using her to meet the terms of his father's will ... Well, as J.S. would say, she'd be out of here faster than a grasshopper out of a chicken yard.

Trouble was, he didn't know which bothered him more—using her...or the possibility of having her walk away.

"I've cooked for twenty-five." Becca's voice came to him from a distance.

Kody followed the sound to the kitchen, where he found her opening the light pine cabinets and pulling out drawers. The place looked like a minor disaster area.

"Cast-iron skillets? Cast-iron Dutch ovens? And *whisks?*" Brows raised, Becca shot him a quizzical glance.

More drawers flew open. "A full arsenal of knives including—" she lifted out a lethal-looking piece of cutlery and laid it on the Mexican-tiled countertop "—a Sabatier knife?"

Again she turned to him, brows knitted into a frown. "All right, where's the rest?"

"What makes you think—?"

"Kody, those pots belong to J.S. They've got his initials marked on them. But I'll bet he doesn't use whisks or top-grade French knives. I'd bet my first week's paycheck this kitchen had gourmet cooking equipment before you moved in. Am I right?"

He scowled. "Bunch of shiny stuff. Not much good on a ranch. I didn't want J.S. wasting his time cleaning it. I told him to sell everything he wouldn't use. He needed a new saddle," he added gruffly.

"Oh."

For a moment she was quiet, absently sliding things back into drawers and cupboards while she studied him with those unsettling silver-green eyes.

He rasped the hoarseness from his throat and started back toward the dining room. "Supper at six. The men expect it on time." He needed to escape the close confines of what he used to think was a pretty big kitchen.

"Hold it. Let's see what I'll need from the store." She opened the freezer door. Out came one frozen package after another. "Beef, beef, *beef?*"

"Becca—"

"I can see we're going to need lots of chicken. And some fish. Ah, here's a package of trout, but I'll need more."

"Becca, the store—"

"What about vegetables?" She closed the freezer door and pulled open the other side of the refrigerator. "I hope your cook keeps lots of fresh vegetables on hand because—"

"*Rebecca!*"

Silence. He could almost hear its roar. She turned, and he saw the angle of her jaw, the flash of rebellion in her green eyes.

"My father calls me Rebecca. You are *not* my father."

Oh, but he wished he were. Then he could issue a few short commands and get the hell out of there instead of standing around like an unsure teenager too damned concerned about her approval.

"Becca," he conceded. "The store is a half hour's drive. There are staples in the pantry over there and a garden out back. Even a few chickens running around if you've a mind to catch one." He squelched a grin, made a point of showing her which door was the pantry. "We don't eat fancy here."

"I see." She studied him again.

The silence extended until he found himself shifting feet. But the resistance faded from her face. What took its place looked disturbingly like the approval he'd been seeking.

She turned back to the refrigerator, leaning in to check its contents.

Suddenly he was aware of her well-shaped, jeans-clad derriere. Swiping a hand around the back of his neck, he transferred sweat from his palm to the seat of his Levi's. Just five more minutes...

"Okay...good." The refrigerator door bumped shut and she headed to the pantry, where she went through the same examination. The contents must have passed muster, because she snapped the door closed behind her.

"I think I can manage—"

"Then I'll get back to work." He all but bolted toward the dining room.

"Good. I'll check the rest of the kitchen myself."

That brought him to a reluctant stop. "What rest?"

"Like what's behind these other doors." She had that look that said she'd rummage on her own till she saw everything.

"That's a closet." He pointed her attention away from his bedroom door. "Luce keeps cleaning things in there. Mops...brooms, stuff like that."

"And the other door?" She smiled up at him as if she'd just asked about the weather.

The weather was growing steadily worse. "My room," he growled. But not for long. As of tonight, he'd be sleeping in the barn.

Becca crossed her arms and leaned against the butcher-block island, waiting for Kody to leave. How was she going to get anything done with him fussing like a mother hen?

Correction. Definitely not a hen. Kody was more like a large bear worrying over an intruder in his den. She needed to get rid of him before she did something rash.

"Fine. You can get back to your cows now."

His answer fell somewhere between a growl and a grunt as he strode toward the dining room. "Supper at six."

Thank goodness. Becca slipped the scarf from her ponytail and tied it back tighter. Now she could get to work. Start figuring out how she was going to rescue herself.

She lugged a cast-iron pot up onto the stove and stared down into it. How was she going to cook in big black pots like these? How was she going to become self-reliant with Kody shadowing her every move? How was she going to remember she had only *temporarily* postponed the wedding?

How was she going to resist looking into his room?

Strictly off-limits, she told herself, clanging on the pot lid. Snooping did not fall into the realm of innocent curiosity.

On the other hand, knowing what cleaning equipment was available did. A cook should be prepared to clean up after herself, shouldn't she? Relieved at having a simple goal, she marched to the closet.

The door squeaked as she swung it open, and a clean pine scent assailed her nose. Inside she found brooms, a graying cotton mop, a bucket, a laundry hamper. A plastic tool carrier sat on a shelf in the back filled with . . . what? On tiptoe, she peered in to inventory the cleaning products.

"You could see better if you had a light."

Her heart lurched. She whirled as light flared from an overhead bulb.

"Kody!" He loomed in the doorway like a dark mountain, so close she could feel his warmth. "You practically scared me out of my skin."

He retreated two steps, but not enough to lessen the heat that seemed to fill the closet.

"Sorry."

He didn't sound sorry. He sounded angry, and he looked as if he'd like to be out digging fence holes or busting a bronco or pulling cactus spines out of his hide. Anything less painful than standing where he was.

"If you need help, you should ask for it."

"But I don't need—"

Before she could finish, he reached for the plastic carrier. The small space filled with the earthy scent of hard work and leather, and when his chest brushed her shoulder, she felt something like a shock. Suddenly she was on sensory overload, breathing in his presence, hearing the pounding of her heart, feeling something tickle the side of her neck.

Kody was all gathered brows and set chin and scowl as he backed away. Unable to breathe, she brushed at her neck . . . felt the tickle travel up her wrist.

Out of the tangle of her feelings, it came to her that sensual reactions did not have little feet!

"Spider!" Squealing, she twisted away, shaking the small black insect from her hand. She watched the creature spin itself down a silken bungee cord until it reached the floor and skittered straight toward her.

"Eeeee…" She scrambled backward into a solid wall. Too late, she realized the barrier was far too warm and pliant to be the butcher-block island.

She practically jumped away from him. "Oh, Kody, I'm sorry. It's just that I'm a little—"

What she saw in his eyes only added to the pounding of her heart. Exasperation. Anger. Something dark and smoldering.

Move, her mind shouted. *Put distance between you and whatever haunts this man.* But her legs didn't seem to be working. They were turning to noodles, and all because of this bear called Kody. She'd knocked off his hat, backed him up against the butcher block and made him positively fume.

But all she could think of was what he would do if she reached up and kissed him.

Chapter Three

Kody couldn't move. Becca was hardly bigger than a colt, but he felt as if she held him captive against the butcher-block island. He watched bewilderment and surprise widen her dusty green eyes, and he had to clench his teeth down hard at the sight of her full lips. They were pursed and slightly open—as if she were about to say no.

A delectable mouth. Wearing the shape of a kiss. No man should have to withstand temptation like this.

Already beyond good judgment, he closed his hands around her arms and watched her eyes grow more confused. If she stopped him now, he might still have a chance. But she didn't, and he knew he was lost.

She felt so small in his hands, so...precious. He wanted to taste her sweetness, to feel the smooth silkiness of her lips, to breathe in the elusive scent that was with her everywhere she went. He wanted to kiss her.

The first time he had ever seen her, his traitorous Sanville passions had imagined how her kiss would be.

"Kody...?" Her textured voice held the sound of leaves in the wind, fluttering and uncertain. As if she had imagined kissing *him*.

Suddenly she stiffened, and her gaze darted to his shoulder.

"Kody, the spider!"

"No!" Before she could swat the insect, he closed his fingers around her slender wrist. The contact was like touching velvet petals in a sun-warmed garden. Like feeling the hum of honeybees in the current of her pulse.

Except that he could sense her fear. Following her anxious gaze, he spotted the spider scrambling up his sleeve. He offered his other hand to the tiny creature, coaxing it onto his finger where it began a slow trek up his hand.

Becca gasped, a soft intake of air that raised the hair on his neck. He could feel her wanting to pull away, and he had to fight the storm threatening his own heartbeat.

He didn't want to let her go. Everything inside him shouted to take the kiss still shaping her lips. But he knew what he had to do.

Reluctantly, he released her wrist and strode to the back door, carrying the tiny black insect with him. He laid his hand on the back porch rail, and the spider wandered a lazy path down the length of his finger—as if it were taking its time to keep him out of the kitchen...away from temptation.

"You don't need to stall, *Gogyeng Sowuhti*. You've done your job. Are you waiting for a thank-you?"

As if appeased, the spider crawled off his hand and rode a silken cord down from the porch rail.

Another time he might have laughed. The spider was probably just another bug trying to reclaim the ranch house land. He could sympathize with that. But if she *was* the Hopi goddess of his mother's stories, she had managed to do what he couldn't. She'd brought him to his senses.

If he were smart, he'd hightail it as far away from Becca as he could get. And not show up for supper. But he owed her some kind of an explanation. And he needed his hat.

Reluctantly, he stepped back into the kitchen and found her standing at the sink. What struck him first was her long hair, tied in a blue scarf, brushing the back of her pale blue shirt like a sheaf of rippling gold. The sight weakened his intentions.

"I . . . uh . . . owe you an . . . explanation."

"No you don't." Her voice rasped like corduroy. She didn't turn around.

"Look, in Hopi beliefs, the spider is called Spider Grandmother. The Hopi believe she looks after them. Helps them through hard times."

Spider Grandmother makes impossible tasks possible. How many times had his mother told him? He'd gotten through some pretty difficult tasks in his thirty-one years. He'd get through this one, too. As long as he remembered the differences between Becca's world and his.

Spider Grandmother helps her people with decisions on which their fate depends, his mother had taught him. Was it a fateful decision to hire Becca? More like *fatal,* if he didn't absolutely swear to keep from kissing her.

Becca sniffed. "It's okay, Kody. I understand. Ranch hands have to live with bugs."

"Are you okay?"

She turned then, and her eyes sparkled with moisture. Wrinkling her nose, she snuffled against her fist, offered a shaky smile and tried to blink away tears.

"Of course I'm okay. I'm just peeling onions." A shimmering drop overflowed one eye and tracked down her cheek. She caught it with the back of her wrist and wiped it onto her jeans. "Don't you think you'd better go back to your cows?"

He hesitated. All afternoon he'd been trying to get away from her. Now her tears made him feel like a damn deserter.

"Right." He spun around and was halfway to the door before he remembered. Three long strides and a silent curse carried him back to his hat. Snatching it up, he settled it on his head, tugging it low over his eyes. "Supper at six," he growled one last time—then beat it out the back door.

"Onions!" That was the mildest of the words he spat out on his trek to the barn. Becca *wasn't* crying—she'd said so herself. In spite of being as small and wide-eyed as a fawn, she'd felt solid and sturdy in his hands. There was softness—*damn* the word—absolute velvet in everything about her. But there was determination, too.

There had better be, by damn. He scuffed his boots for emphasis, raising clouds of dust with every stride. Becca had *asked* for this job. It *wasn't* up to him to make it easier. He *shouldn't* be trying to protect her from spiders. He *shouldn't* be worrying about her peeling onions.

If he wasn't careful, it would take more than a Hopi goddess to make him remember all that.

Becca scraped the chopped onions into the big cast-iron pot and breathed in the sharp, sweet aroma as they sizzled in hot bacon grease. A mound of cubed beef followed. She shoved the chunks around, stirring until her arm ached. Blotting the sleeve of her denim shirt against her moist forehead, she clanged the heavy cast-iron lid on top.

The concoction smelled good. She would make it *excellent*.

At the sink, she shoved her shirtsleeves up and scrubbed the onion from her hands, rubbed them dry on the red-checkered towel, then blew her nose.

Damn Kody, anyhow. For coming back into the kitchen. For catching her in the closet. He'd startled her, that was all. He'd stood way too near, and she'd overreacted to that silly little spider, and then he'd held her, and then . . .

Bits of things Trey had told her about Kody came trickling back. How Kody's Hopi heritage made him respectful of all living things. How the Hopi believed they were the earth's caretakers.

Becca's spirits threatened to tumble again. She'd tried to kill his Spider Grandmother. How mortifying.

Kody had acted as if the spider had more right to be here than she did. It hurt to admit he was probably right. To him she was just—what had he said?—a soft city woman. He didn't really want her here.

Yet she'd wanted him to kiss her.

She searched the kitchen for a box of tissues, gave up and used the hand towel to blot her eyes. Of course there'd be no tissues here. Real men didn't use tissues. Real ranch hands didn't cry . . . not even while chopping onions.

She pitched the towel into the hamper in the closet and vowed she wouldn't shed another tear. She hadn't grown up with four impossibly irritating brothers for nothing.

She wouldn't let this quiet, smoldering man overwhelm her.

And she wouldn't let herself be attracted to him!

She'd show Kody she could manage on her own, and she'd start with the best damn chili he'd ever eaten. Lifting the pot lid, she stirred the browned meat, then added the rest of the ingredients, finishing with scoops of chili powder.

Only one way to tell if it was okay. With a small spoon, she scooped up a sample. Ummm...pretty bland. These were cowhands she was cooking for here, not her "soft city brothers." From the *ristra* hanging above the butcher block, she cut a red chili pepper, chopped it fine and stirred it into the mixture.

There. Macho chili.

Now all she had to find were the makings for a big green salad. Maybe a pie for dessert. Simple enough. If she couldn't find fruit, she could always make chili cobbler.

It wasn't until she was carrying the big white soup bowls to the dining room that she realized she was humming.

Somewhere in an outlying room of the ranch house, a clock chimed a melody that seemed comically British for a New Mexico ranch. A series of sonorous bongs accompanied the arrival of three cowboys. They straggled into the dining room looking defenseless and exposed without their hats—hung on the pegs in the entryway, Becca supposed. Their damp hair lay slicked back from foreheads that were startlingly white compared to their sun-browned faces.

The tallest looked like Ichabod Crane, Becca thought, struggling for a little humor.

Darn it, why did Kody have to be late on her first night, when she didn't even know the supper routine? Apparently neither did the men, because two of them slouched against the sides of the arch studying their boots while "Ichabod" studied her.

Well, somebody had to take charge. "Won't you sit down, gentlemen? I'm Becca Cov—"

"Rebecca Covington, men. She'll be cooking till J.S. is back on his feet."

In spite of all the resolutions she'd made that afternoon, Becca's heart jumped. Kody strode into the dining room on the last fading chime of six o'clock, but having him there made her more nervous than if he were still missing.

And she couldn't stop looking at him. He was hatless, like the other men, and deeply bronzed, from the opening of his shirt to his hairline. His coal black hair glistened with drops of water, and as he neared, she caught the sharp scent of soap. He was so ruggedly masculine. Yet he cared about the life of a tiny little insect.

"What are we waiting for? I'm hungry enough to eat a saddle blanket." He pulled out the straight-backed chair at the head of the table. Two of the men moved to stand at the long bench on the left, but "Ichabod" held back. So did she.

Kody looked up. *"What?"*

"Well, boss, since J.S. isn't here . . . ?"

Kody's gaze shifted from the cowhand to Becca. "Sit where you always do, Ike. Becca, you sit next to me. Ike Kramer there, Ed Wagner and Tully Turner on the other side."

"Ma'am," they greeted her, a trio just slightly off-key.

"Please call me Becca." She smiled. "And please, do sit down."

The long benches scraped the hardwood floor as the men slung legs over and settled in. Kody sat down last. No one moved to start the food. The men stared at Kody, but he seemed mesmerized by a big white platter of sliced tomatoes.

Suddenly Becca realized he was waiting on her. Quickly she lifted the lid from the pot in the middle of the table.

"We were plumb out of saddle blankets today, guys. I fixed chili instead."

A muffled snort told her she'd tickled at least one rib, but Kody didn't look up.

"Why don't you help yourselves while I bring the salad." She laid the ladle at Kody's place, willing her hand not to tremble. Then she fled to the kitchen.

Standing in front of the refrigerator, she pressed a shaky hand to her mouth. Oh, God, what if they didn't like the food? What if they didn't loosen up? What if Kody refused to look at her through the whole meal?

"Hey, Kody, where'd you find the new cooky? Make a mighty nice blanket partner."

A rumble of laughter in the dining room sent heat racing up her already warm neck. She opened the refrigerator door and tried not to listen, but the temptation was too great.

"Hot *damn!* Better try the chili before you change her job. If this was any spicier, she'd have to put it on ice."

"This's the best chili I ever ate."

"Better bring more bread, Miss Becca. This here chili needs a little cushion."

The men's humor and a generous dose of refrigerator air calmed her a little. Straightening the collar of her fresh pink blouse, she pulled out the salad.

She was being ridiculous. This was just a meal . . . just a temporary job. No matter how Kody acted, she had no reason to be nervous. In fact, the more withdrawn he became, the more independent she could be. The easier it would be to put him out of her mind.

Back in the dining room, she climbed into the spot Kody had assigned her. Dipping from the pot, she filled her bowl and dug in. And stifled a startled gasp. Beads of perspiration broke out above her lip and across her forehead. She'd had no idea how powerful a dried chili pepper would be.

Across from her, Tully mopped his forehead with a red bandanna. "Great chili, Miz Becca. Tad spicier 'n J.S.'s."

The men laughed.

"Salad's good, too."

"I made peach cobbler for dessert."

Ike whistled through his teeth.

Kody didn't say a word, but she noticed he took seconds.

When they'd finished, she cleared the table and returned with the pan of peach cobbler still warm from the oven and richly fragrant.

"You serve, Kody. I'll get the coffee." She set clean plates in front of him and held out a knife and spatula. Darn him, wasn't he ever going to look at her?

He took the utensils and studiously cut the first piece, full of golden peaches, thick with sugary syrup.

Shifting her weight, Becca settled in. The meal had gone okay. The least he could do was to acknowledge that, and she wasn't leaving until he did.

Kody scooped the serving onto a plate, handed the knife and spatula to Ed, followed by the pan of cobbler. Resting his forearms on the table, he frowned up at her. "Didn't you say something about coffee?"

Becca's bravado slipped. She must have breached some ranch-table custom by asking him to serve his own employees.

"Coming right up." She flashed a smile loaded with false assurance and hurried back to the kitchen.

"Man, this is great cobbler!"

Carrying the glass pot from the coffeemaker across to the stove, Becca poured coffee into the big metal pot.

"But you know what J.S. says. 'The purtier the gal, the worse coffee she makes.'"

The men's laughter knocked more wind out of Becca's confidence. They didn't teach how to make *cowboy* coffee in her high school home economics class. Probably she was supposed to put rocks or oats or some other secret ingredient into that big metal pot along with the grounds . . . and then cook the dickens out of them. But maybe the four extra tablespoons she'd put in the electric brewer would make it strong enough that they wouldn't notice the difference.

She wrapped a towel around the metal handle and lifted the pot from the stove. Squaring her shoulders, she carried it back to the dining room like a banner into battle.

She started with Kody—she wasn't stupid. He'd made it clear he was the boss. She wouldn't make that mistake again.

Liquid, black as tar, swirled into his white mug, and with it the last of her courage. The coffee looked ghastly!

Kody waited until she'd filled the other men's cups. "You'll have some too, won't you?" His voice was almost cordial.

"Of course." She could feel the men's eyes on her as she poured her cup full and slid into her place. Ignoring the knot in her stomach, she raised her mug.

"Well, guys, here's mud in your eye." Over the rim she watched them raise their cups.

She made herself take a tiny sip.

Lord! Mud in the *mouth!* But maybe ranch coffee was supposed to taste like this, if she had any luck left at all.

A strangled gag told her what she already knew—nobody could be that lucky.

Kody coughed. Set his mug down hard. For a moment, he stared at it as if he expected toads to hop out.

Becca didn't dare take her eyes from the dark liquid sloshing over the rim of his cup. Seconds later, she winced when the screen door slammed. Now she knew what ranch coffee *wasn't* supposed to taste like.

"Uh, pass the cream, Miss Becca." Ike nudged her with an elbow and pointed at the squat white pitcher. "Sugar, too, please."

A weak smile was all she could muster as she handed him both. He stirred them into his cup until the contents swirled a sickly beige. Ed and Tully followed his example, their silence broken only by the earnest clanking of spoons.

Almost in unison, they raised their mugs and tossed back the mixture. Just as quickly, then pushed away from the table, clattering spoons and rasping benches in their haste.

"Great supper, Miss Becca."

"Yeah, thanks. You're a mighty purty cook."

"Uh, Miss Becca...no coffee for me in the mornin'." Tully disappeared through the archway.

"Me, neither," the other two echoed. Then they fled.

Becca sat at the table staring at the muddy liquid in her cup, trying to ignore the ache of discouragement in her chest. Hemlock would look more appetizing.

Her first meal had been a terrific success. The ranch hands said they liked her chili, they'd warmed up enough to kid her, and they'd eaten every last bite of her cobbler. Those sweet men had even choked down her coffee and given her a compliment—so she wouldn't feel too bad.

Right. The truth was, she was a lousy ranch cook. Her chili was too hot, her coffee was ghastly and she was afraid of spiders. And the more she was drawn to Kody, the more she seemed to irritate him.

He'd probably send her packing before sundown.

She sniffed and swiped a fist under her nose. Maybe she'd be wise to just go.

Kody made his way across the hard-packed earth from the barn to the back of the house. He told himself he was taking his time because it was getting dark and things on the ground weren't all that easy to see.

But he knew better.

He'd behaved like an irritable old bear at supper. He'd been surly and judgmental, and he owed Becca an apology. Her first meal had been better than he'd dared hope. And bad coffee was easily remedied.

But, damn, he had to find a way to be around her without this powerful pull of attraction. He had to ease the guilt of deceiving her. He could at least tell her about the boys.

Somehow, he had to find harmony with Becca, because treating this woman badly was inexcusable.

Nearing the house, he glanced up, hoping to find the kitchen light on and her slender form moving around inside, doing the things women did to make a place a home. But the windows peered back dark and uninviting, forcing him to a hesitant stop.

He didn't want to talk to her upstairs in that room. The pretty, feminine bedroom was just another place where he was too much aware of her, where he felt rough-edged and out of sorts. Another world where he didn't belong.

Maybe he'd talk to her in the morning, help her make coffee before breakfast. In the interests of harmony.

He paused on the porch step and drew in a deep breath. Faint traces of a hauntingly familiar scent teased his nostrils.

"Becca?"

"On the top step." Her soft, textured voice stopped him from coming further.

"I didn't see you there."

"I didn't think you did." She sounded almost wistful.

"Thought you might've turned in already."

"I wanted to listen to the night."

Her words made him aware of the sounds, the long, rasping screech of a barn owl, the dancing music of a cricket, the bawl of a calf somewhere in the distance. The silence in between.

And the undertow of sadness in Becca's voice. It tightened a knot in his gut.

"About dinner, Kody. If you want to try to find—"

"That's what I was coming to talk to you about."

The silence expanded, became a barrier where before it had been a flow.

"The meal was fine, Becca. I should have told you." Pretty damn weak for an apology, but he wasn't trying to win her favor. Only give her the credit she deserved.

"Thought I might give you a few pointers on the coffee."

The silence extended. He could almost feel her withdraw, knew it was probably for the best. Her boots scraped, and she pushed up out of the shadows, stood straight-backed above him in the darkness.

"From the way the guys doctored theirs, I guess I could stand a few lessons."

Her voice had changed. The wistfulness was gone, replaced by a raspy brightness that sounded more like bluff. And a laugh that had lost its sparkle.

"No time like the present." She took the last step up and fled toward the kitchen. A light flashed on, flooding through the screen door, making Kody squint as he followed her inside.

She stood at the sink, pulling the inner pieces of the big metal coffeepot from the drainer at the side. "I've never made coffee on the stove before—"

"Becca." He had to resist the urge to move beside her, to take the metal parts of the pot from her hands so he could quiet her fluttering fingers between his. But that wouldn't quiet his own throbbing pulse.

"What?" Her expression turned suddenly defensive.

"We only use that pot if the power goes out. Or when we're on the trail."

Now was the time to tell her about the trail—about the boys and The Journey. But he found himself digressing, taking the easier route.

"There *is* a trick to making good coffee at a camp fire. You have to promise you won't tell J.S. I shared his secret."

The resistance in her eyes eased a little. "I promise."

He allowed himself to move a little closer. "What you do is crack a whole egg into the grounds." He stopped to appreciate her wrinkled nose. "Then toss in the shell..."

Her brows rose in beguiling disbelief.

"And boil the whole thing...just long enough. The shell makes the loose grounds settle to the bottom."

"Sounds awful." She attempted a smile, but her dimple remained hidden.

"It makes a great cup of coffee." *On-the-trail coffee.* He should be telling her what her other chuck-wagon duties would be. But he couldn't bring himself to break this moment of harmony.

Becca picked up the dishcloth and pushed it around the bright Mexican tiles of the countertop. "Kody, how is J.S.? Has he had the bypass surgery yet?"

"They decided not to operate. Did an angioplasty instead—that little balloon procedure? They'll send him home in a couple of days."

Becca's hand stopped. "Is he going to be okay?"

"Callie said he'll be fine. He just has to learn to take things easier."

She hesitated. "Are you sure she'd tell you..."

He saw it then, a fleeting flash of sadness. Trey had told him of their mother's death little more than a year ago. Becca was still grieving.

For the first time, he let himself smile, just enough to show he was sorry for her loss. "I'm sure Callie would share whatever she finds out. J.S. is a cantankerous old buzzard, but she knows he's the closest thing to a father I'll ever have.''

He'd hoped to lighten the mood, but her eyes answered with something different. Hurt, deep and unexpected. And anger. Just as quickly, her feelings were hidden by long cocoa lashes that cast tiny half-moon shadows on her cheeks. She fingered a small gold knot on a chain around her neck.

"I'm sure you'll be relieved when he can come back to work." Her voice had become distant. She folded the dishcloth and laid it on the counter, then lifted dishes from the drainer and carried them to the cupboards.

"He won't be back for a while. In the meantime, I'm glad you're here." It was as close as he was going to get to an apology. To comforting her.

Her gaze flew to him, wide-eyed and openmouthed with surprise. He wanted to take her in his arms and kiss her until the dimple in her cheek deepened with a real smile.

Instead, he grabbed a handful of dishes and carried them across to her.

She stiffened noticeably. "I can do that." She snatched the dishes from his hands and loaded them into the cupboards.

"You should have used the dishwasher."

Her head tilted slightly, and a faint frown appeared between her brows. "There weren't enough dishes to fill it. Besides, I wanted to do them." She fled back to the sink.

"Will you stop a minute so I can show you how to use the coffeemaker?"

She spun around, hands fisted at her sides. "Kody, I know how to use a coffeemaker."

She reminded him of the little yellow tanagers he sometimes saw up in the mountains. *Sikyatiti*—yellow bird—in the language of his mother's people. If he wasn't careful, Becca would flit away as quickly as the birds.

"Okay, Becca." He looked beyond her to the door to his room. He didn't really want to sit inside and listen to her work. Didn't want to be in such close proximity to Becca and his bed at the same time.

"Uh, maybe you should go up to your room early. It's been a big day for you, and you look a little tired—"

"Kody, are you my boss...or my keeper?" Anger flared her slender nostrils and gathered her tempting lips into an unconscious pout. "Thank you very much for the coffee-making lesson." She snatched an iron pot from the drainer and slammed it down on the stove. "I'm sure if I ever get the urge to go camping, I'll be the Julia Child of the wilderness." The lid followed the pot, clanging on top like the bell for the first round of a fight. Becca looked as if she were ready to go all ten rounds.

"I don't need any more of your help, Kody, and I *don't* need you telling me when to brush my teeth and when to go to bed. We're talking grown-up woman here. *One who can take care of herself.*"

She turned back to the sink, her shoulders stiff, her wavy hair reaching down her back as her chin lifted. "If you want another cook, I'll be out of here in the morning." Her voice held a soft, unsteady sound, as lonely as moonlight on a rippling river.

His own anger flared then—he didn't know why—but he grabbed it like an eight-second bull and hung on. Becca was more woman than he'd let himself dream of, but she was *bahana*...and a Covington. He never should have let her come here.

Before he made the mistake of going to her, of turning her around and looking down into those enticing green eyes, he hung on to the bull of his anger and rode it all the way to the back door.

"I'm not looking for another cook. Good night."

He let the screen door slam behind him and skimmed down the steps into the darkness, away from the house and the forbidden Rebecca Covington, before he said what he really wanted to tell her.

No, Yellow Bird. I don't ever want you to leave.

Chapter Four

Why hadn't Kody fired her?

Restless and distracted, Becca wandered down the front steps of the ranch house, grateful for the sun on her shoulders toasting away the early morning chill. What she really needed to answer was why she had practically invited him to let her go.

Straying around the side of the house, she welcomed the diversion of the ranch scene—the windmill, the two mules at the silver-gray stock tanks at its base, the big metal barn next to the corral. She had studied the barn through the kitchen window last night, a clean-cut beige building that looked as deliberate and costly as everything else at the ranch. At least it gave her somewhere to go. She set off with an uncertain sense of purpose.

Figuring out why Kody hadn't fired her didn't exactly take a Phi Beta Kappa key. He had probably decided last night's meal had been at least edible and he'd have to settle for that. Thank goodness breakfast had turned out better. She smiled, remembering how Ike had hung around for a second cup of coffee and complimented her on her biscuits.

But she knew the real reason Kody hadn't told her to pack up. J.S. wouldn't be gone all that long, and trying to find another cook would be more trouble than it was worth.

At the corral, she rested a boot on the bottom bar of the metal fence and squinted up at the windmill, motionless against a cloudless blue sky.

If she was totally honest, she knew, too, why she wanted Kody to fire her. Because she wanted him to kiss her.

Last night, she'd decided she should leave. Spider Grandmothers and bad coffee were probably bad omens, and being in a lonely room in an empty house wasn't an improvement over living with the hovering men in her life. But then she'd heard Kody moving around in his room below, reminding her that the house wasn't empty, that the man who slept downstairs was the real reason she wanted to leave. And the reason she wanted to stay.

Everything about Kody seemed to make her want. And she didn't know what to do about it.

Except get busy. She pushed away from the fence. Time to stop tilting at windmills and get busy doing...something. She would focus all her errant emotions on the ranch. She'd learn everything there was to learn. Stopping in the wide barn doorway, she peered into the shadows. "Hello? Anybody in here?"

Wings fluttered overhead and a fly buzzed by.

She stepped inside, shivered at the cooler air, breathed in the satisfying smell of horses and leather and hay. But the stalls appeared to be empty.

From somewhere nearby, she heard soft, muffled cries, irresistible animal sounds that lured her down the concrete aisle and through an open stall door. In the far corner in a pocket of straw lay a black-and-white cat with a squirming litter of kittens. Delighted, Becca crept nearer.

The cat raised her head and yowled the bristly warning of a protective mother.

"It's okay. I won't hurt your babies." Kneeling, Becca reached toward them. "They're so beautiful," she crooned.

The cat didn't protest when she gathered up a fuzzy black ball. Its sharp little claws dug into her hands, and its frightened mews made her cup it against the front of her shirt to stroke it gently. She hummed soothing words until the kitten curled against her and the vibrations of its purr tickled her hands. The sensation made her smile.

"They're barn cats, not pets."

Only Kody's voice could send her pulse soaring. Struggling for calm, she straightened slowly, still cuddling the kitten against her midriff.

He was standing just inside the stall entrance holding a coffee mug.

"Why is it you keep scaring the wits out of me?" She spoke quietly, still crooning, hoping her pounding heart wouldn't disturb the kitten.

"Why is it you're in a place a cook doesn't need to be?" He sounded angry.

From the mound of straw, the mewlings grew louder, mixed with a meow from the mother cat.

"I wanted to see more of the ranch." Becca looked back at the kittens—anything to avoid Kody's disapproving eyes. To her amazement, a tiny, black-and-white ball of fur wobbled shakily across the floor straight toward him.

The mother mewed insistently, and whatever she had to say jolted Kody into action. He strode past Becca, eyes hidden in the shadow of his hat, and knelt near the cat. Carefully he poured the contents of his cup into a pie tin hidden in the straw. Milk.

"She's lame," he growled, "but she breeds good mousers." In one gentle gesture, he scooped up the stumbling kitten that was trying to reach him and cupped it in his free hand—much longer than indifference would have allowed. Then he laid it back in the circle of its mother's paws.

Embarrassment, that's what she'd seen in his eyes, not disapproval. She'd shown up in the wrong place at the wrong time and become an unwelcome witness to his care.

What a mystery Kody was—all hard angles and toughness on the outside, with such gentleness underneath. And an intensity that made her tremble.

"I'll take that one, too. They shouldn't get used to being petted." He stepped nearer and reached out for the kitten she still sheltered.

Too aware of his nearness, Becca held back, stroking the tiny bundle in her hands. She didn't want to give it up. The kitten was already learning to trust her. She didn't want it to become as skittish and unapproachable as Kody.

A kitten in her room at night would make it less lonely. A kitten would help her be less aware of the man downstairs.

"Kody, couldn't I just keep—"

She'd meant to make a simple appeal, but when she looked up, the words stalled in her throat. Kody was more than frowning—he was waging a battle. His gaze locked with hers, commanding her to hand over the kitten and get the hell out of there. At the same time, his head tilted closer.

She felt his breath on her cheek, and all she could do was look up at him, waiting, as if the very day had stopped. Then his mouth brushed hers, and wanting, sharp as flame, shot through her. He leaned into the kiss, testing, tasting, caressing her with his mouth. Touching her only with his mouth. A soft mewling whispered between them, and she didn't know if it came from the kitten or from her own lips.

Her limbs turned liquid and weak, and she thought she might melt slowly to the ground. She wanted to slide her hands around his neck and pull him to her, to feel the length of his body and the touch of his hands. Yet she couldn't let go of the kitten, couldn't tell anymore which of them purred.

And then it was over. Kody pulled away, and she knew she must have fallen from an airplane. The thrill lingered, but the fall was devastating.

"Kody...?"

His head jerked up. "Keep the kitten. You'll be responsible for it."

She could feel his anger, could see resistance in the black depths of his eyes, and something that looked, incredibly, like regret. But it was gone before she could trust she'd really seen it. That dear, familiar V settled between the dark lines of his brows.

He sucked in air, as if dragging in fortitude. "Go back to the kitchen, Becca. If you don't have enough to do, make roses out of radishes."

* * *

Thwack! The ax bit deep. A splinter of wood thudded onto the pile of chips surrounding the chopping block in the middle of the clearing.

Kody yanked the ax free, savoring the smooth slide of the handle through his right hand as he swung the blade back up over his shoulder.

"Uh!" The blade split the log deeper, the force of the blow reverberating up his arms and through his chest. The impact felt good. The growing soreness in his muscles and the perspiration rolling down his back—they all felt...necessary. Whatever it took to exhaust the flames that still consumed him, to get rid of these damning Sanville passions. He would chop logs until he dropped, until he burned away all thoughts of Becca. All memory of the kiss he'd taken.

Jerking the ax free, he swung again. With a resounding crack, the log split, and he threw the pieces to the pile at the side of the clearing. Symbolic acts, he knew—the fierce rending, the casting away. He needed Becca at the ranch—he needed the pretense of a wife-to-be. But he'd torn away from her kiss, and he would stay away from her from now on.

From the pile of logs yet to be split, he chose his next victim and leaned to heft it up. At the sight of Becca, he almost broke rhythm. She stood at the edge of the clearing, arms folded across her sun-colored shirt, dappled by the light dancing through the cottonwood leaves overhead. She looked like a forest princess. She looked determined.

Somehow he managed to heave the big log onto the block without faltering. In the distance a dog barked, and nearby horses' hooves drummed, yet being there with Becca in the clearing felt far too intimate.

Suddenly he wished he hadn't shed his shirt, that sweat hadn't tracked down his torso to soak the band of his jeans. He wished he couldn't feel her watching him.

"Kody, I don't do radishes."

He swung the ax high and buried it deep into the ancient rings of the log, fighting his guilt. Refusing to look up at her, he worked it free for another attack.

"I'll have time between meals. I could be doing other jobs. I could help with the cows."

If she hadn't spoken with such innocent appeal, his ax never would have wobbled, but he remembered her holding the tiny kitten, and it wasn't much of a stretch to imagine this soft Covington woman caring for a newborn calf. The picture was twice as devastating.

But not a smart digression with a sharp weapon in his hands. The blade swung wide, slicing a splinter into the air. Fear forced his gaze to her, to judge the danger of the unintended spear. Relief followed as it fell short of hurting her. Just as quickly, his reaction turned to anger.

"Know a lot about cows, do you? Want to work with heifers, too? Steers? How about bulls? Maybe I should put you in charge of the culls." He hoisted the ax again.

"I don't know what a cull is, Kody, but I'm not stupid. I can learn."

This time the ax cut true and deep, slicing away what he'd intended. But somehow the satisfaction was gone.

"There's not enough to do in the kitchen, and I'm sure J.S. has other things he's responsible for. Why can't I do his other jobs so he won't be behind when he gets back?"

Damn. If she threw another question like that, he'd wind up a half-footed half-breed. Chopping wood had suddenly become hazardous instead of healing. He thumped the ax down and grabbed his shirt, swiping it across his forehead and around the back of his neck.

Stalling for time. But he couldn't afford to put her off much longer. Even if it meant she'd quit, he had to tell her about the boys who were coming next week. He had to tell her about The Journey.

Becca stuffed her hands into her pockets and tried not to watch. Thank goodness Kody was putting on his shirt. It was bad enough standing here remembering that he'd kissed her—even if it was the most undecided, unfinished, *unbelievable* kiss she'd ever experienced. But to watch him chop wood in that half-naked state was more than a healthy, red-blooded woman should be asked to do.

Of course, Kody hadn't asked. He obviously had no idea what effect he had on her. The clearing seemed to heat by degrees as she watched him slide knotted, glistening arms into the sleeves of his denim shirt and tug it on to absorb the sheen of his sculpted shoulders and back. He even left the buttons undone. She tried not to follow the rivulets of sweat tracking down his sleek chest.

He was as beautiful as a glistening bronze statue. With Levi's and a ponytail! She half smiled, then caught herself, still wondering how he would feel under her fingertips. Quickly she clenched her hands into fists.

"So what do you say, Kody? You don't want J.S. to have extra work when he gets back, do you?"

Kody put the ax away and rescued his hat from the branch of a tree. His eyes tacitly avoided her.

"Come on, Kody, what are some of J.S.'s jobs? Why are you holding back on me?"

His hands hesitated in midair before he settled his hat where it belonged.

"Kody, what aren't you telling me?"

"No more than you're not telling." Long strides carried him out of the clearing.

"Like *what?*" She dashed after him.

"Like why you wanted this job?"

"Because I . . . I like to cook and—"

"Fixing grub for guys who spend most of their time talking to cattle?"

"With J.S. out sick you needed—"

He rounded on her then, staring down with anger she didn't understand. "I don't need a guardian angel." His frown deepened, and he loomed tall and indomitable. But something yielded in his eyes, as if his pride were losing a battle. "Trey said you just finished a master's degree," he growled. "I doubt it was in animal husbandry."

"It wasn't. But I've always been good with—"

"Money? That's what Covingtons are good with, aren't they? Probably a vice presidency is waiting for you right now at the family bank."

If he'd sounded as if he meant it, she would have fought back. But underneath all that dark disapproval, she sensed something else. Something strangely like regret.

Don't make me do this, Kody. Don't make me own up to being worse than you imagine. Her fingers touched the delicate twist of gold on the chain around her neck. *My family wouldn't even tell me my own mother was dying.* Her eyes stung with anguish. *I'm not a soft city woman. I'm the Covington baby.*

No. She swiped a fist under her nose and jerked her hat down hard. She would not let Kody treat her the way the men in her family did. That's what being on his ranch was all about. She had to learn to take care of herself.

This time, it was she who strode away, setting her course toward the ranch house. "I asked for the job because I . . . I've always wanted to be a cowgirl."

In a few long strides he caught up with her. "Riding a horse at a fancy Eastern stable isn't like working cattle."

"I know that. But Trey and I used to dream of having a ranch. Like yours. I thought the job would give me a taste of it before I go back to the real world."

He swung around in front of her, feet wide apart, his hands suddenly hard on her shoulders. "The *real* world?"

A tremor slammed through her at the disapproval that flashed in his eyes, like sparks struck from black flint.

He must have felt it, because he dropped his hands as if he'd touched fire. But the flames didn't leave his eyes. "So this is sort of a vacation for you, right? A little outdoor adventure before you get back to the cold, cruel world of country clubs and BMWs and summers in Nantucket." Irony tinged his voice.

"I'm sorry, Kody." She resisted moving her shoulders and shook her head instead, trying to forget the heat of his touch, to escape the intensity of his gaze.

"It was a bad choice of words. I just want to do some hard outdoor work before I go back to . . . a job in the city. I won't be working for the family bank." He'd think she was a bleeding heart if she told him she wanted to work with underprivileged kids.

"You want some hard outdoor work?" He glared at her a moment more, then turned back toward the barn. "In a couple of weeks, we drive the cattle to summer pasture. J.S. is in charge of the chuck wagon . . .

organizing supplies, driving it into the mountains, setting up camp, feeding everybody.''

Becca almost had to trot to catch up with his long strides. That had to account for the way her heart raced. "I can do that, Kody. I could start planning right away. How many will I be feeding? Do you use a pickup for the chuck wagon?''

"We use a chuck wagon for the chuck wagon.'' He cut around the corner of the barn.

At the sight that greeted them, Becca stopped dead. Angled at the side of the metal building stood an enormous wooden wagon, like something straight out of an old Western movie. A spindly looking bench spanned the front, four exposed hoops arched over the body, and what looked like a large chest of drawers sat on the back.

"Ranches still use these things?''

"Not all of them do, but this one does, and the cook is in charge. Along with looking after the animals and playing nursemaid to the boys.''

"The . . . *boys?*''

"Yeah.''

It was his hesitation that brought her attention back to him full force. She watched him circle the wagon as if he were taking inventory. Or avoiding her.

"Five of them. Kids who've never seen a country club, never heard of Nantucket. Kids who've already bumped heads with the law.'' He kicked a spoke on a rear wheel. "They'll probably need more herding than the cattle. They might not take to a pretty, pint-sized slicker.''

Kody was doing it again—making her mad and melting all her defenses in the same breath. Who would have thought his care for earth's creatures included delinquent kids?

This must be the job Callie Keams turned down.

This was the job Becca wanted.

It would be perfect—the very kind of work she'd gone to school for, but now she could do it on a ranch. She could become independent and self-reliant right along with the boys.

All she had to do was convince Kody.

"My degree isn't an MBA, Kody. It's an MSW. I was planning to work with disadvantaged kids back home."

She held her breath while he studied her. He looked so skeptical, she might as well have told him she had a degree in UFOs. "Growing up with four insufferable brothers was pretty good training, too." She tried for a convincing smile, but it wilted under his disbelieving scrutiny.

He completed the circuit of the wagon and veered off toward the corral. "Okay, Becca, tell me what degrees you have to handle Mo and Sory." He waved toward the two mules standing in the crisscrossed shadow of the windmill like a pair of long-eared bookends.

"One of the men will drive the wagon, but you'd be in charge of them the rest of the time. They're pretty bullheaded critters. Might not take to a woman."

"They can't possibly be any more stubborn than the men in my family." She must have sounded angry, because he turned to scrutinize her again.

"Kody, it doesn't take a degree to manage mules." As long as she was granted a few little miracles along the way. "But the boys... they'll need nurturing. I can pass out salve for saddle sores, and I can wrap a mean Ace bandage when it's needed. But I can help with wounded spirits, too."

He turned away. The muscle along the straight line of his jaw knotted, and his broad forehead creased above his finely chiseled nose. He looked as if she'd touched alcohol to an open wound. Whatever he struggled with, she wanted to reach out and comfort him.

Being on the trail with five young boys who demanded all her thoughts and energies was the only way she would survive this man. On the trail, she and Kody would never be alone. She wouldn't be able to listen for his sounds in the night. She could get over this little infatuation she seemed to be suffering for the lonesome, struggling cowboy.

"I want you to give me a chance at this job, Kody."

He pushed away from the fence and opened the wide gate.

"Okay, Becca. We'll do it on a trial basis. Two days from now, J.S. was to take supplies up to the summer cabin and get it ready. Do you want the job?"

She swallowed hard. "Well...sure. If someone can tell me what needs to be done. And give me directions." She drew in a shaky measure of air and followed him into the corral.

Kody was trying to scare her off, but it wouldn't work. Going into the mountains with a couple of stubborn mules for company wasn't exactly her first choice for a lesson in self-reliance. But the mules would be a whole lot easier to be with than Kody.

"Maybe Ike could fill me in."

"I told you, the men all have their own work. I'll be giving the instructions."

Kody didn't look at her. She was afraid to wonder why.

"And I won't be sending a woman up to the cabin alone. Especially not overnight."

Chapter Five

"Overnight?"

Becca watched Kody stalk the two wily mules around the corral and breathed a sigh of relief that he was too busy to notice her panic. *Was he planning to come with her?*

"It takes a day to haul stuff up to the cabin. We'll head back the next morning." He barely raised his voice, as if he were explaining to the mules instead of to her.

Watching him communicate with the animals, Becca's alarm eased a little, tempered by growing regard. Kody was as patient with the mules as he'd been gentle with the kittens in the barn.

"When we take the kids and cattle up, we'll move a lot slower." Shifting deftly, Kody snagged the halter of the larger animal. "We'll spend at least a couple of nights out on the trail with them."

Kody continued to talk, a kind of quiet cajoling just between him and the mule. She couldn't make out his words, but the deep murmur of his voice calmed her. Warmed her.

Unfortunately, his manner didn't have the same effect on the mule. Ears back, the beast raised his head and locked his legs, refusing to move.

"Okay, Becca. Here's your first job—hang on to Mo while I capture Sory. Maybe you two can get acquainted."

Becca pulled herself up to her full five foot five and took the animal's halter. She felt very small next to the long-legged animal. Kody was probably trying to scare her off again, this time with a cantankerous, oversized critter.

But Kody didn't know she'd never been afraid of horses.

Ears still back, Mo jerked on the rope, curling his lips to reveal flat yellow teeth that looked threateningly big.

Becca grinned back at him. Big old Mo didn't know he was as much horse as jack. From her jeans pocket, she offered a lump of the sugar she'd brought in case she found some horses.

He eyed her warily, then reached to take it in his lips.

"Atta boy." She breathed a slow sigh of satisfaction.

Across the corral, Kody patted the other mule's neck and led it toward her. His gentle treatment only served to renew her alarm. She'd rather spend a month in the mountains with spiders and coyotes than spend one night there with Kody. As it was, she'd need every minute of the next two days to figure out how she'd survive.

Kody reached for Mo's halter. "I'll take him now."

The animal jerked back.

"Okay, you stubborn old coot." Kody's words hummed with affection. "Just stay here with Becca,

then. I'll be back as soon as I get Sory hitched." He led
the bigger animal out of the corral.

Becca huffed in disgust. Did Kody think she couldn't
even lead a mule? She tugged on the halter rope. "Come
on, Mo, give me a break here, big guy." To her amazement, the animal yielded, following her around the barn.
Whether he missed his buddy or hoped for more sugar,
she didn't care, so long as they showed Kody she could
manage without his help.

At the sight of her with the mule, Kody paused while
slipping the bridle over Sory's head. "Whatever you did
to get that animal moving, I want you to show me."

Spotting another bit and bridle on the wagon, Becca
set to work with Mo, trying to steady her nervous fingers. "I'll trade you for a lesson in hitching up the
wagon. That way I can do it on the trip by myself."

She knew Kody was still watching her. The intensity
of his gaze made her fingers falter, made her scramble to
finish the job.

He mumbled something that sounded a lot like "may
lightning strike me," then slid a collar and harness onto
Sory and backed the animal into place at the front of the
wagon. He ran a palm along the mule's brown withers
and reached up to scratch a long ear. The animal grew
calm under his touch...at the same time Becca's temperature rose.

She hadn't noticed Kody's hands before, but she saw
now that they were big and powerful, and at the same
time gentle. Kody handled animals with extraordinary
care. Would he treat adolescent boys the same?

How would he handle a woman? The question slid
into her awareness before she could stop it, making the
fine hairs on her arms erupt.

Ridiculous. Outrageous! Chafing her arms, she willed the sensation away.

"All right, Becca. Let's get Mo hitched."

She forced herself to watch him, tried to memorize the steps of the procedure. In no time, the animal was in place, and Kody swung up to the driver's seat.

"Put your foot on a spoke and give me your hand."

The same square hand that had gentled the mules closed around hers. Somehow she endured the rough warmth of his touch, though heat spread through her. She felt as if she were floating.

But the sensation didn't last. No sooner had she sat than the animals lurched forward, jolting the wagon into motion, nearly rocking her off the seat. Instinctively, she reached for balance, then felt Kody's arm tense under her grasp. Snatching her hand away, she steadied herself on the thin metal armrest and willed her heart to stop pounding.

Kody glanced at her sideways, that rare flicker of amusement dancing across his face. She stifled a retort equating men and mules and refused to admit that she was pleased.

Metal springs squeaked, and the seat rocked as Kody steered in a zigzag path around the open area behind the barn. The wagon felt as if one good bump would shake the whole caboodle into a pile of so many weathered boards.

"Is the trail into the mountains this...bumpy?"

"No." He shot her another quizzical look. "It's worse. Full of rocks. Lots of holes. Big tree branches. Takes a pretty experienced driver."

Experienced at what? she wondered. At riding up here without touching shoulders, the way Kody was doing? At keeping from sliding across the inches of space he managed to maintain between them? Under these circumstances, her heart would never stop racing.

"Then I'd better start learning." She'd have to learn to manage these two ornery mules behind this overgrown picnic basket, because she sure couldn't ride up here beside Kody for two days. She'd just end up trying to finish that kiss he'd started.

"Okay, Kody, I'm ready to try it."

This time he looked straight at her. The humor was gone from his eyes. "You're not driving."

"But *why?*"

"Because. These are difficult animals and mountain terrain is rough and they need a stronger hand than—"

"Than a *soft city woman's?* How do you *know* if you don't let me try?" How did he expect her to learn to become anything else?

The long, tense silence was broken by one gruff word. "Fine."

But he didn't sound fine at all. She could read all his misgivings in his darkening eyes, see all the uncertainty that deepened the V between his brows.

"Here." He handed her the worn leather straps.

They shifted in her hands like flat, heavy snakes trying to slither out of her control. She gripped them tightly, sure she'd rather wrestle a couple of copperheads. Controlling the mules and driving the wagon frightened her, but the job dwarfed next to the thought of riding beside Kody. Somehow she'd just have to manage.

"Loosen up on the reins. Same as on a horse. Give them some slack. Let them know you're in control," Kody commanded.

But she *wasn't* in control, least of all of her confidence. If there were such things as guardian angels, she hoped hers were helping, because she wasn't sure how else she was going to get through this.

Same as on a horse. She *did* know how to ride a horse. Tentatively, she reined the mules to the right. The wagon began to turn.

They responded. To her!

Using a bit more control, she steered them toward the vegetable garden. The mules executed a wobbly circle all the way around, sending a couple of chickens squawking away.

She was doing it, driving the chuck wagon. She felt like hollering "Eeeee-haw!"

"Look out, chickens. Wild lady driver."

"Kody Sanville, I am not—"

He was almost smiling. For the first time, she saw approval in his eyes. The sight turned the words in her throat to bubbles of laughter.

She snapped the reins, and the mules picked up, breaking into a run toward the front of the ranch house, making the seat rock and roll, jouncing her against Kody. She relished an aftershock of elation. Maybe later she'd let herself think about why.

Right now she concentrated on getting around the corner of the house without a sideswiping incident. Careening to the front, she calculated the circle she'd have to steer to stay away from the big black car parked by the porch.

"Give me the reins."

Suddenly she felt the brush of Kody's hands as he reached to take them. He looked as stern and disapproving as she'd ever seen him. The bubbles buoying her spirits burst, but stubbornness tightened her grip.

"Kody, *why?*"

"I forgot. I have a . . . business appointment. I want you to get off. Go start lunch."

She pulled back steadily on the reins, praying the mules preferred a nice lazy walk to a headlong run. The animals slowed, and she relaxed a little.

"Becca . . . give me the reins."

"If you have an appointment, it makes more sense for you to get off." She tugged again and the mules came to a stop.

Holding the straps tightly, she scooted her bottom toward the middle of the seat, deliberately bumping Kody. "You go meet your appointment. I'll drive these guys around back."

He scooted away from her. "No. I won't leave you alone with these unpredictable animals."

She shifted another inch and bumped him again. "Then I guess you'll have to meet your appointment right here, 'cause there's a man in a suit getting out of the car and he's looking this way."

She wasn't sure if her last scoot pushed him off or if he chose to catapult over the side, but she couldn't mistake his muffled curse. Couldn't keep from grinning.

Kody deserved to be annoyed. He was as bad as her overprotective brothers. Probably worse.

Standing by the wagon, he glowered up at her. "Drive them back to the barn. *Slowly*. No side trips and *no* racing. Just stop behind the barn and leave the reins on the ground. I'll be back to take care of them later."

A car door slammed, and he swung around. The man in the suit was mincing his way in their direction as if he were trying to avoid walking on dirt. He raised one hand in a shaky wave.

"Go!"

When mules fly, she thought. A macho command deserved a smart retort—even if he was her boss. But he was already striding away across the wide space, covering twice as much ground as the man coming to greet him.

Curious, Becca watched them meet at a point near the house. Kody shook the man's hand, but something about his manner told her this wasn't his usual welcome.

"Okay, guys." She turned her attention back to the mules. "Time to mind our own business. What say we amble on back to the barn like we know what we're doing?"

The mules' ears pricked up, but she held back on the reins and allowed herself another glance at Kody. He and the man climbed the porch steps, then turned in her direction. The man in the suit waved again.

Was he someone she knew? Maybe she should drive over and find out. She looked for some sign from Kody. He raised his arm and smiled, but even from this distance, she could tell it wasn't real.

She raised her own hand to answer, then understood that Kody wasn't waving at all. He was motioning her away.

Whispering a small prayer to the guardian angels of mules, she shook the reins. Mo and Sory jerked into motion.

Thank goodness. She concentrated on willing the animals in the right direction. As they turned the corner of the ranch house, she allowed herself one last glance back.

Kody and the suit were still standing on the front porch. They were still watching her.

* * *

Kody cursed. What in the name of all the Hopi Katchina spirits was going on? The wagon rested in its usual place behind the barn, and Mo stood by the water tank in the corral, eyes closed and his tail switching. Sory was nowhere to be seen.

First Becca had disappeared after lunch, and now his mule? Just one more worry to add to his already foul mood.

Kody hadn't expected his father's attorney to show up so soon. He hadn't realized how badly he would react when the weasel asked to meet his "pretty little mule-driving bride-to-be." It had taken all his control to get the man off the place diplomatically—instead of just throwing him off.

Kody tramped to the wide barn entrance and stopped stone still. What the...? "Becca, what are you doing?"

"This is called grooming, boss." She smiled up at him, continuing to brush the mule's hip, working her way to his thigh. Her jeans tugged tight across her backside, and wisps of wavy blond hair feathered around her face, escaped from the green scarf at her nape. She looked feminine and inviting. Next to the big animal, she looked almost elfin.

The mule's muscles twitched under her touch, and Kody fought a groan. Sory was practically in a trance, and damned if he didn't look like he was smiling. Not a scene Kody could watch much longer without a serious reaction.

"Kody, I don't think these animals have had a thorough grooming in a long time. Just look at this tail."

This time he did groan. "This is a ranch, Becca, not Pimlico. Mules don't get racehorse grooming. No wonder Sory looks like he just died and went to heaven. You're going to ruin all my animals."

Another reason why he should do what he'd decided during lunch. He was going to give her her walking papers, get her out of here—before the attorney had a chance to talk to her, before she figured out Kody had deceived her. While he still had an ounce of self-respect.

He'd tell that smarmy shyster Griswold that Becca had broken their engagement. He'd find some other way to beat the terms of his father's will.

"I see the wagon's back in place. I thought I told you not to bother the men for help."

"I didn't. I unhitched the mules myself. It took some negotiating, but the three of us finally arrived at an understanding. I think we'll do just fine on the trail."

How could he continue to act like such an ogre when she was so pleased with everything she accomplished? This little woman wasn't bigger than a tumbleweed, looked as delicate as spider's silk, yet she was proving all his judgments of her wrong. She was too much like sunshine breaking through his storm clouds. He couldn't let that happen.

"When you finish, put the mule in the corral." He turned away, stunned by his cowardice. It was a simple-enough task, telling her he was sending her back to Vermont. Nothing like when he'd been a kid facing down a gang of East Coast *bahana*. But he couldn't bring himself to face *her*.

Later. He'd tell her later. Just before he left to take supplies up to the cabin. He'd send her packing, then escape into the mountains alone. He'd forget everything he'd discovered about her, this *bahana* woman who was all the things he'd vowed he'd never want.

He strode outside and made it almost past the chuck wagon before she caught up.

"If you have time, I'm ready to learn about the trip."

Though she made a show of inspecting the old wagon, somehow she managed to be in Kody's way no matter where he turned. Pleasure brightened her face, and in spite of all his resolve, he was glad she'd come after him.

"Tell me about the chuck wagon."

In the face of her interest, his resistance lost more ground. "Got it at a farm auction in Mora. Thought it would be more fun for the kids than a truck."

She circled slowly, looking and touching. Stopping at the old wooden barrel, she ran fingertips along the tarnished metal bands. "What's this for?"

"Water."

She wrinkled her nose. "Isn't there a cleaner way to carry it?"

The sight of her pert little nose gave him another flash of pleasure. "It has a plastic liner."

She lifted the wooden lid to peer inside, and came up grinning. "Your basic rough-and-ready office watercooler. Quite a cover-up. Is there a refrigerator and a microwave in the back, too?"

"'Fraid not." The only other cover-up was his, and he would end that soon. Before Becca found out. "Everything in the chuck box runs strictly by fire."

"Chuck box?"

"Chuck box." He unlatched the hinged door across the back of the wagon and swung it down, resting it on the support leg to form a worktable. This was what he'd come out to check in the first place, not a pretty woman with far more mettle than he'd given her credit for.

"It's like a traveling pantry!" Becca reached into the shelves, touching the contents as she had at the house—

tin plates and cups, knives, forks and spoons, a collection of pots and pans blackened from a lifetime over camp fires.

Kody had to stop watching her exploring fingers. Bracing a foot on the rear bumper, he hauled himself up to the chest of drawers sitting above. The wagon groaned with his weight, then creaked again, and he felt it make another adjustment. Then Becca appeared, standing in the wagon bed, grinning at him over the top of the chest.

She looked tremendously pleased with herself . . . and completely delectable. He yanked out the top drawer to distract her attention. To keep himself out of trouble.

Becca rested her elbows on the chesttop and leaned across to peer into the drawer. Her soft, wavy hair fell forward over her shoulder.

She was so close, so tempting. Even balanced precariously on the bumper, Kody caught himself leaning toward her, breathing in her faint fragrance. Like a fool rushing in for another kiss.

But she didn't seem to notice. She was too busy rummaging through the containers in the drawer.

"Ah-ha, nursing supplies." She lifted out a tin marked with a faded red cross and sorted through the contents. "You'll have to help me with a list of things to buy. Horse liniment, heat rub. And we'll definitely need a teddy bear."

That was enough to bring him at least partially back to his senses. "No stuffed toys!"

Becca's eyes widened.

He took the tin from her and dropped it back into the drawer, closing it with a slam. He refused to be captured again by her sweet innocence. The Journey was to teach the boys confidence and self-reliance, not to run for comfort to a stuffed animal.

He needed to fire her right now, before she came up with any more of her softhearted ideas. Instead, he yanked the second drawer open, rattling the empty metal containers inside. Silently cursing himself for his cowardice.

"Oh, good. Canisters for staples." Becca shuffled the labeled tins into order. "Beans, coffee, flour, rice, sugar. This gives me an idea of where to start."

He couldn't let her start *anything*. "Becca, about the job—"

An engine rumbled nearby, and she straightened, sweeping her tumbling ponytail back behind her shoulder.

Torn between relief and exasperation, Kody let his attention be tugged away by the pickup rounding the corner of the ranch house. Ike must have a posse on his tail because he was leaving a billowing wake of dust.

Kody jumped down from the chuck wagon just as the truck braked to a crunching stop nearby. From the driver's seat, Ike jackknifed his lanky legs out onto the ground.

"I got the list from J.S., and the stuff's in the back." Ike's attention strayed to the top of the chuck box. "Thought I oughta bring it right on out to the wagon, seein's how—

"Well, howdy, Miss Becca." He snatched off his hat and squinted up at her with the silliest grin Kody had ever seen.

"What's the hurry, Ike?"

The tall, angular man twisted his hat in a circle and glanced back up at Becca. "Well, boss, it's just that that Mr. Griswold called and—" His eyes followed Becca's retreat from behind the chest.

Kody heard her jump to the ground.

Ike leaned toward him furtively. "Griswold said to tell you he'd be back tomorrow mornin'—*early*." His voice had dropped to a hush. "Said he wanted to meet *everybody*."

Kody's adrenaline kicked in with a rush. Griswold didn't want to meet *everybody*. He wanted to meet Becca. He'd assumed that Becca was Kody's fiancée, and Kody hadn't corrected the idiot's assumption.

Becca appeared from behind the wagon. "Did I hear something about supplies?"

Kody glared at his watch. Not enough time to get Becca to the airport in Albuquerque left today. Not if he meant to fire her without hurting her.

Griswold had left him no choice.

"Okay, we've had a slight change of plans. Becca, go pack yourself a backpack. Ike, let's get the truck unloaded. We're leaving soon as the wagon's ready. Won't be back for at least five days."

Chapter Six

Five days. Five days. Five days.

Becca rocked on the wagon seat, listening to the mules' hooves clop-clop on the trail leading to the summer cabin. Their steady rhythm didn't soothe her worries away.

Neither did the scenery. The rolling landscape blooming with bushes of buttery lace and the pine-covered mountains beckoning cool and green under a vast blue sky should have been the perfect setting to stir a sense of glorious freedom...and the independence she longed for.

But the whole five days she'd be with Kody.

Under the shadow of his white hat, Kody still looked all hard angles and shielded thoughts, as he had ever since they'd left the ranch that afternoon. He reined his restless white-gold horse to a prancing walk yards ahead of the wagon.

"Get those mules moving, Becca."

"I thought you said the trip took only two days. I don't see why we have to hurry if we'll be gone for five."

At least he'd agreed to let her drive the wagon—a truly major concession. She knew it wasn't because he thought she was a good driver. A traitorous little voice inside kept whispering—*It was because he didn't want to ride beside you.*

"Steer those animals off to the side."

Great. Now he was ignoring her *and* giving orders— like a hard-nosed trail boss from the movies. Darn it, she was supposed to be learning to challenge this kind of treatment.

"Why should we bounce along on the side when there's a perfectly good trail?"

"So the mules will get used to it," he called back.

She'd never make it through five days of this. "Kody, I want to learn and I don't have the chicken pox, so will you stop trying to carry on a conversation from the next county."

That won her a glance, but the flash in his dark eyes unsettled her more than his indifference.

"The wagon travels *off* the trail to keep distance from the 'point.'"

"So what's the *point?*" she shot back, challenging him with the obvious pun.

He reined his horse around and stopped. One brow cocked upward. "The point is to keep dust out of the food."

Was he teasing back? She blotted a rolled-up sleeve to her damp forehead to cover her uncertainty. The farther they traveled, the more the tension seemed to grow between them.

"The 'point,' Becca, is the rider in the lead, the target the cattle follow."

There was no mistaking his intentions now. He was explaining things to her like her brothers did when they were treating her like a dumb *girl*.

"Okay. Off the trail." She steered the mules from the worn path and scolded herself for a serious lapse of purpose.

Hard work, that's what she was here for, and wide-open spaces. They would be the cure for whatever she imagined sparked between her and Kody. She just needed to remember one thing—his kiss had never been part of her plan. But standing up for herself was.

"You didn't tell me why we're in such a hurry."

Nudging his horse, he moved ahead again. "I want to make it as far as possible before dark."

"Oh." She'd forgotten that part. If she'd had trouble listening to Kody's night sounds at the ranch, how would she possibly handle them under the stars? Keeping her attention on work would be a lot more difficult once the sun went down.

She cleared the feathers from her throat and started over. "Tell me what it will be like with the boys."

The mules' hooves beat steadily, and the old wagon creaked. She waited, wondering if he would answer. Slowly the wagon rolled beside him, and she realized he'd slowed so she could catch up. But he kept his gaze in the distance.

"We'll set off early in the morning. Just before light. When the calves are all mothered up." He glanced at her. "That means staying close to their mothers. They're easier to move that way."

His voice had deepened and warmed a little, and the lines at the corners of his eyes softened. Nudging back the brim of his white hat, he gazed up at the mountains. "Each day we'll drive to a higher pasture. The boys will bring up the rear. They'll eat a lot of dust." A corner of his mouth tugged upward. "Teach them the meaning of true grit."

His unexpected humor weakened her determination.

"Kody, I worked with delinquent boys during college—kids with their 'hood' colors and their hip-hop language. Their different baseball caps even had secret meanings. Kids like that might not take to being treated so rough."

Layers of emotion darkened his harsh laugh. "Rough is all these kids know. They don't fit in, don't have anywhere to belong. They're fighting the whole world, and a soft heart and teddy bears won't help."

Teddy bears. Her suggestion must have touched something painful. "Everybody needs something to love, Kody, even if it's only a pet. Especially these kids."

"A pet won't keep them out of jail, and that's where most of them are headed. Unless somebody turns them around."

Learning to love would turn them around, but that didn't strike her as a topic she wanted to pursue with Kody.

"Okay, so what if they refuse to work?"

"They'll work...the first day because they think cowboys are tough. After that, they'll work because they'll have to prove to one another how tough they really are."

For the son of a wealthy New Mexico rancher, Kody seemed to understand delinquent boys pretty well.

"Riding behind the stragglers is an easy place for them to start," he continued. "Teaches them responsibility. Teamwork." He paused. "Besides, greenhorns *always* start there."

"It's a wonder you haven't assigned *me* to ride back there," she murmured.

He turned to look at her then, squinting one eye almost closed. "I haven't made all the assignments yet."

She saw it again, that endearing flash of humor. This time he *was* teasing, and it made her heart flutter.

"I didn't know this trip was an audition. What other tortures do you have planned for us greenhorns?"

A devilish smile threatened to undo his scowl. "You'll face scorching heat and teeth-grittin' dust. Rain and lightning. And the nights get freezing cold. You may get charged by a steer. Even bitten by a snake."

She inhaled sharply, then caught him fighting a grin. *"Kody!"*

"You'll wear the same clothes until you want to burn them and you'll wash in the stream—after you break the ice."

He was having fun with her now, trying to scare her with his spaghetti-western miseries...and enjoying every hair-raising detail.

Something warm and yearning flared in her at the sight of the half smile that played around his mouth and laughed in his eyes. Clearly, he was describing a life he loved—a challenging, adventurous life. A life of independence.

Kody was a real cowboy, the kind she'd once dreamed of loving.

Kody dismounted near a cluster of aspens and dropped the horse's reins to the ground. "Pull the wagon to the other side of the clearing, Becca. We'll stop here."

"Good."

The sharp relief in her voice sent guilt shooting through him. He should have stopped an hour ago—

before dusk set in. He'd pushed her far too long. But he still hadn't figured out how to handle the night that lay ahead.

Becca steered the mules beside a stand of pine trees and jumped down to attend to their needs.

All afternoon, she'd handled the mules like her personal pets. She'd driven the wagon as if she'd been doing it for years. So far, everything he'd given her to do she'd managed like a champion. Every time he thought he'd found a job she couldn't handle, she'd proven him wrong.

"Is it the cook's job to start a fire? Because if it is, I'll need a flashlight to find wood."

His guilt exploded at the tired determination in her voice. "*I'll* fetch the wood. You start the food." From the wagon he lifted out two kerosene lanterns and struck a match to their wicks. A circle of light pushed back the rapidly encroaching darkness.

Lowering the grub-box door, he propped up the worktable and hung one of the lamps above. With the second lamp in hand, he headed toward the trees. "I'll have a fire going long before you're ready to cook."

That was the way to do it—toss out a challenge. Keep her busy. The same method he would use with the boys to keep *them* out of trouble. He stooped to gather kindling.

Work and more work, until they were ready to drop. Until he had no energy left to think about Becca. Laying the small branches by the fire pit, he stalked back into the trees.

Exhaustion—that was the key. He made several more trips, collecting a sizable pile of dead branches on the forest floor. *They'd both fall right to sleep, on opposite sides of the fire.*

Right. And prairie dogs could sing. He stood at the edge of the clearing, captured by the sight of Becca's face in the honeyed glow of the lantern flame. She'd hung her hat on the side of the chuck wagon, and light danced on the loose strands of hair that haloed her face.

In daytime she was like sunshine. She brought brightness and laughter into his life, qualities he barely remembered experiencing before. But at night? How could he have known what she'd be like at night on the trail? She was like an alluring, golden flame.

He was going to have to get very, *very* tired.

Scooping up a huge armload of wood, he aimed for the fire pit.

"Oh, good, you're back." Becca joined him at the circle of rocks, a frying pan in one hand and a pot in the other. She was grinning—an impish look of delight. "I'm ready to cook, boss. So where's the fire?"

He dropped the wood with a grunt. How could she still be wearing that faint, sweet scent after so many hours on the trail? How could she be so...cheerful? A good wood-smoke fire would take care of both in a hurry. He hunkered down in front of the pit and began layering the kindling.

"Want some help? We had to do this at camp every summer." She set the pots down and knelt beside him, reaching across for larger branches.

All she did was graze his hand, but she might as well have brushed him with flame. Heat flashed through him in spite of the chill in the air, and sweat broke out on the back of his neck.

Just as quickly, she was on her feet, fumbling in her jacket pocket. "I found matches. I'll just leave them here and get the coffeepot." Dropping the box, she hurried away.

"Hold it!"

She stopped at the edge of the lantern's light.

He forced himself to soften his tone. "No coffee. It's too late for coffee."

It took her a moment to answer. "You're right." Then she was off again, but not before he caught sight of something new in her eyes, something questioning . . . and shy.

Had she felt it, too—this tension between them, so charged and compelling?

He ground out a sharp oath. No, it wasn't Becca. It was his inheritance, this swell of desire. His father had discovered innocence, had inflamed and overpowered it. And taken. Only to abandon the reality that followed.

Kody wouldn't let that happen to him. Nor to Becca.

He slammed a large branch hard against his bent knee and focused on the pain. Adding the broken pieces to the kindling, he struck a match and held it to what he'd built. The flame curled the dried grass into black spirals and caught on the small twigs.

In the light of the rising fire, Becca returned to settle the pots into place on the rocks.

"I'll get dishes." Kody fled to the wagon where he found her scent still lingering, waiting to make him forget what he'd come for. Standing by the chuck box, he got lost in watching the firelight dance around her lithe figure as she bent to stir the food.

Plates. Flatware. Reason! Angrily, he dug through the storage shelves, pulling out what they would need. He clanked the utensils together and moved reluctantly back to the fire, knowing any man in his right mind would go to his sleeping bag hungry rather than spend more time with Becca.

It didn't help when she settled on the log across from him. Elbows on her knees, she balanced her plate of beans and ate as if she'd spent her life around a camp fire. Yet for all that, she still looked soft. Delectable.

Damn. He was aware of everything about her, the saucy way she'd turned up her jacket collar to ward off the chill, the way her lips puckered when she took a bite of food. He couldn't stop watching her.

"So, Kody—"

A log shifted in the fire, making a shushing sound, and her eyes darted to check it.

"I'll wash the dishes while you put the canvas over the wagon. In case it rains." She glanced upward. "Oh!"

The word was no more than a soft intake of air, but it raised hen flesh on his neck. He followed her gaze to the blue-black sky, hung with flecks of light that reached out forever. A shiver crept up his scalp at the wonder of it, at the realization that Becca might never have seen such a sky.

"It doesn't *look* like rain, but you never know." In spite of her cavalier tone, her voice sounded more textured and throaty.

His neck shivered all over again at the soft rasp.

"I don't want to get wet."

He almost choked on a mouthful of beans. He swallowed hard. "Becca, trail cooks don't *sleep* in their wagons."

On the other hand... He downed a gulp of water. This might be the very solution he'd been looking for—Becca closed in the wagon, like a princess behind locked doors. Why hadn't he thought of it?

Because J.S. and the rest of the men would laugh him all the way to Sunday if they found out. He shouldn't make exceptions for Becca. Everyone had to rough it on the trail.

He shouldn't make exceptions for himself. He'd just have to tough it out tonight.

"The wagon isn't to sleep in, Becca. The cook sleeps on the ground, just like the rest of the crew."

"Oh." She sounded worried.

"You'll get used to it." But would he? "Soon as we clean up, I'll show you how to fix a comfortable spot."

Who did he think he was kidding? There was no such thing as a comfortable spot on the trail. Especially with Becca nearby. He *knew* how it would be with Becca curled up beside him. Unfortunately, *comfortable* was not the word that leapt to mind.

"We've got a lot of ground to cover tomorrow. Soon as we clean up, we'll turn in."

That way he'd have lots of time . . . to lie awake wishing he were anywhere else but here.

How was she ever going to get through the night? Becca squirmed in the sleeping bag, trying to redistribute the thick mat of pine needles Kody had layered under her tarp. They'd make a nice, soft mattress, he'd said. More like a layer of frozen peas if you asked her, and she didn't think it was because she was a princess.

She didn't feel like a princess. She felt like a very unhappy Covington. Tears stung the corners of her eyes, and she fought them back angrily. She'd been pampered all her life, which was why she was so tired and cranky now. She wished she could just crawl over and slip into Kody's arms and be comforted the rest of the night.

But she absolutely would not even think that thought another second. She couldn't imagine a better way to make a complete and utter fool of herself. And that would be nothing compared to how she'd feel when he growled and sent her away. She wouldn't give him another chance to do that.

She just needed a day or two to get toughened up, that was all. She would show Kody that this Covington could be as self-reliant as any self-respecting cowhand.

Grabbing the side seam of her jeans, she gave a giant tug and flipped herself onto her back, then smothered a moan of frustration. The middle of the sleeping bag was wrapped around her like a wrung-out towel.

"Is something the matter, Becca?"

Kody sounded far away and muffled, but his dark silhouette still hulked like a small range of mountains behind the spirals of smoke drifting from the fire pit.

"No." Yes! Her feet were cold, and her tarp lay over three large boulders that poked her no matter where she moved. Her shirt was wrapped halfway around her neck, and she wished she had on her nightgown. Her hair smelled of smoke and she was keeping Kody awake and—

"Do you ever see skies like this in Vermont?"

He sounded nearer now, maybe because he sounded more...friendly. She opened her eyes and looked straight up.

Above, the whole universe shone with stars, some so near they begged to be touched, others beyond even the reach of dreams. Like Kody.

She took a deep breath. Tried to let go of her frustration. "Back home the stars look like a layer of dots. Here they're like..."

"Like what?"

He would think she was silly. "Like silvery cosmic confetti. Like a glorious celebration." She listened for a snort of ridicule, but it didn't come. Slowly she let herself relax, aware of Kody's steady breathing on the other side of the fire.

"There'll be a full moon in a couple of nights," he murmured. "Thunder moon, that's what my— That's what it's called in July."

She was too much aware of him. The break in his words sounded as if he'd bumped into a wall he didn't want her to cross. Even his scent, caught in the folds of the sleeping bag he'd loaned her, reminded her that she was here...and he was over·there. Thoughts like these only made matters worse.

"Kody, can I ask you a question?"

"Ummm."

"If your father didn't work the Sanville Star, how did you become a cowboy?"

In the silence that followed, the dying fire hissed. Crickets trilled and aspen leaves chittered in the night wind. Somewhere a river rushed through the forest, and a hoot owl moaned his repetitious cry.

"Kody—?"

Something thumped nearby. She tried to sit up. "What was that?"

"Probably just a mouse. The forest is busy at night."

"That sounded like a very big mouse. Are there larger animals around here?"

"Fox. Deer. I've heard people tell of cougars. Even bear, but I haven't seen any. Don't worry, Becca. Just watch the stars and go to sleep."

Just go to sleep. She bit back a shaky retort. When she asked him personal questions, Kody's silence was deafening, but his words came quickly enough when he was telling her what to do. Trouble was, right now, she didn't want to be self-reliant *or* independent.

She just wanted to be held.

* * *

What was Kody supposed to do when all he could think of was Becca lying on the other side of the fire—alone? When all he wanted was to take her into his arms?

Becca shifted, and the zipper of her sleeping bag buzzed. "Kody? Are there really bears in these—"

"Probably just a skinwalker." He needed to put more distance between them. He needed to remind himself of the differences between their worlds.

"What's...a skinwalker?" She didn't sound all that anxious to know.

"I'll tell you a story a Navajo friend told me. One evening he was gathering his sheep, when he saw a figure above on a ridge...a dark shape with two legs like a man, but it was bent forward, and its head was shaped like a dog."

She draw in a quick breath. "So what happened?"

"He fired his gun, and it flew away."

"It *flew* away?"

"Yup. The Navajos call them skinwalkers. *Mai tso.* What your people call witches." *Your people.* Harsh words, but he needed to remember them.

"Witches? Kody, you're just trying to—"

"Another friend told me he was driving his truck—a big eighteen-wheeler—up a steep hill. He looked out the window, and a huge man was *running alongside...* wearing a fur coat. Except that the fur still had a head, and it looked like a coyote. Wasn't until the driver got over the hill and into top speed that the man disappeared."

"Did anything happen?"

"No. Just scared him."

He heard a huff of impatience.

"Kody, if you're trying to frighten me with ghost stories, it won't work."

Ghost stories. The skinwalker tales were like that. He remembered how scary they'd seemed to him as a boy.

Suddenly he was aware of Becca's silence. He was frightening her! He could imagine her lying there as still as possible. Listening. Hearing every sound, feeling her pulse leap at each one. He hadn't meant to do that to her.

"Kody, what was *that?*"

He heard it, too—loud, thumping noises, a commotion in the leaves, a rush of wind.

"Kody, something's out there. I can hear it. It sounds like something's after something else."

"There's always something after something else in the forest, Becca. That's the law of nature."

He heard another commotion, this one nearer, just on the other side of the fire. The buzz of a zipper, a rustling, footsteps.

"Becca? Are you okay?"

"I'm sorry, Kody, but if you're going to scare the wits out of me with creepy stories and laws-of-the-jungle reassurances, you'll have to accept the consequences."

He sat bolt upright. Found himself face-to-face with her. She was busy stretching out her sleeping bag...right next to his.

"Now, move over, 'cause I'm not sleeping alone."

Chapter Seven

Chook, chook, chook.

Kody's eyes snapped open and focused on a jay sitting on the high branches of a pine tree. The bird ruffled its feathers and flew away into the pale morning light.

Morning! Kody started to sit up, then froze, listening for the gentle sounds of Becca's breathing. All he could hear was the same harsh call, only louder and nearer.

Damned bird. Scavenging for his breakfast. He'd probably wake Becca, and Kody wasn't ready to face her. Not after last night.

How could he have fallen asleep? It must have been near sunrise when he had—out of sheer exhaustion. He'd spent most of the night fighting the temptation of her small figure nestled against him. Feeling the bow of her back curl into him, breathing in her warm, feminine scent, watching her sleep bathed in the moon's silver light, her long lashes fluttering with dreams—it had all been an incredible gift.

And a damning curse. He'd *had* to stay awake, because all that had kept him from taking her into his arms, from sharing the passion that throbbed through him, was the thickness of two down sleeping bags, and his own teeth-gritting resolve.

He'd wanted her more than he'd ever wanted a woman. But the Sanville passion wasn't enough for Becca. Not even if she wanted him. She deserved more.

Awake and angry, he fumbled with the sleeping bag zipper. He needed to be up and busy before she woke. Pushing up, he found the ground next to him bare. Becca's sleeping bag lay on the other side of the fire pit, folded neatly. As if she'd spent the whole night there.

Was she going to act as if nothing had happened?

He mumbled an oath. How else should she act? Nothing had happened except that he'd scared the hoot owl out of her.

And out of him. Last night he'd realized that wanting Becca was growing beyond passion. She wasn't the pretty confection he'd accused her of being. She was strong and feisty. Eager to try and quick to master whatever he asked of her. He knew in his gut she'd be good with the boys. Maybe better than he. She was smarter, that was for sure.

But he could play it her way—as if they hadn't shared anything last night, not even each other's warmth. Tonight he'd leave her in the cabin. Tomorrow he'd make damned sure they got back to the ranch before dark. Forget spending five days with her—he had to put an end to this torture. He'd send her back to Vermont immediately, before Griswold could meet her.

He fetched his boots from his knapsack, shook them out and tugged them on. An impatient whinny reminded him his horse was hungry. Nearby, the mules stamped and pulled at their ties. But there was no clink of utensils at the chuck wagon, no wisps of fragrance drifting in the air.

Kody stood, kneading his eyes with the heels of his hands, then raked his fingers through his hair. Damn, he could use a cup of coffee. He glanced longingly at the fire pit and discovered a fire already laid. J.S.'s old coffeepot sat on a rock beside the tin of kitchen matches.

The sight actually made him grin. Becca was even becoming a good trail cook. Fishing out a match, he lit the fire and waited for the larger branches to catch and warm his hands. Setting the pot near the flames, he grabbed his knapsack and headed for the stream.

It never occurred to him to track her...not until he slid through a break in the thorny bushes along the bank and caught sight of her at the water's edge. That's when he realized the small bootprints between his feet were hers.

Any gentleman would have turned back—would have slipped away as quietly as a fox—so she'd never know he'd seen her. But he couldn't make himself go.

She knelt at the water's edge, and in spite of the morning chill, she'd shed her jeans and shirt. All she wore were lacy little scraps of underthings that shone like snowflakes against her rosy skin. Her body was slender and lush, like a curving willow branch blooming with plump, silky catkins.

Desire flared in him again, hot and hard. She was like a beautiful forest maiden. As innocent as snow. As seductive as lace. As forbidden as—

She dipped a white cloth into the water, exclaimed as she pulled back from its coldness. Her laugh was a silvery wind chime.

Kody forced himself to turn away. Watching her only increased his torture, because everything she did in his world made him understand how easily she could become a part of it.

He beat a frustrated retreat, trudging ahead, keeping away from the river until he'd worked his way upstream and out of her range. Washing up became the next best thing to a hard, cold shower. He splashed the bone-chilling water across his bare chest and down his back to quench the heat still throbbing through him.

With the cold, damp towel slung around his neck, he tramped back toward the campsite, resolved to put Becca out of his mind.

"Kody, wait up."

He hesitated, then decided to go on as if he hadn't heard. Then cursed himself for considering the coward's way out again. He couldn't avoid her all day.

"Morning."

"It's a wonderful morning." She emerged from the bushes fully clothed, wrestling her backpack to her shoulder. "It's beautiful here. I love the scent of the pines." She looked bright, almost perky, except that she avoided his gaze.

They came to a thicket of trees, and she slipped through, waiting until he joined her on the other side. "You weren't kidding about the water. I almost had to crack ice to get to it." Her face glowed pink from the water's cold, and flecks of moisture glistened in her pale gold hair.

This time Kody had to look away. Becca's sunny disposition was alluring, and yet . . . In the silence that followed, a slow realization dawned. Cheer wasn't an emotion he'd had much practice with, but somehow Becca's cheerfulness this morning didn't ring true. She seemed too absorbed in studying the ground, in avoiding his eyes.

At the edge of the campsite, she came to a halting stop, shifted her pack and tugged her leather jacket down. "Kody, I'm sorry about last night." For a moment, her dusty green eyes met his gaze, then fled to where her fingers fretted with the buttons of her jacket.

"You don't have to apolo—"

"I acted like a tenderfoot. Like a *real* greenhorn. My brothers would accuse me of acting like a *girl*. I...hope I didn't keep you awake."

"No..." She had, but somehow it didn't matter anymore because she sounded like herself again. The undertone of embarrassment only deepened the soft texture of her voice.

"I shouldn't have told those stories. I'd forgotten how frightening they could be."

"You'll be telling them to the boys. I should be able to manage whatever you dish out to them. No special handling. I promise it won't happen again."

No special handling. That's what he'd told himself most of the night...in more or less those same terms. But Becca was making sure he got the message. No special handling of the Covington woman. No handling at all. And she promised the opportunity would never arise again.

Even while delivering a hands-off warning, Becca was gracious, but her words cut deep. Another *bahana* rejection for the half-breed Sanville son... another notch in his tomahawk, he thought bitterly. What better way to stiffen up his spine?

Quickly his pain shifted to anger—at the beautiful morning, at being out here with Becca alone, at the Sanville blood that raged through his veins. At himself for wanting her. He had no right.

Yanking the towel from around his neck, he strode away. "I'm glad to hear it won't happen again, Becca, because there won't be time for coddling on The Journey. Now, rustle up some grub, and we'll get back on the trail."

The wagon rumbled around the last steep turn in the trail and lumbered into a meadow carpeted with wildflowers. At the sight of the log cabin nestled among a cluster of trees, Becca's shoulders slumped in relief.

Thank God. She wasn't sure her backside could survive the wagon seat much longer, especially the way it had rocked and lurched up the trail all afternoon.

But she wouldn't utter a word of complaint. She would never let Kody think she wanted *coddling* again, not even if she had to stand up to one of his skinwalkers. On a moonless night. Alone. Better a scary skinwalker than Kody when he was so withdrawn.

"Pull up under that stand of aspen across from the cabin." Kody trotted his horse past the wagon without so much as a glance.

Not that she was surprised. He'd probably strung together more words just then than he'd bestowed on her the entire rest of the afternoon.

"You got it, boss." Gingerly, she eased down from the seat.

The stern lines of his face didn't change as he dismounted in front of the cabin and stomped over to check the round, white-faced thermometer hanging near the door. From one of the three oil cans standing along the front, he scooped water into a bucket, clanked the ladle back onto a nail and offered the water to his horse.

He was still angry, even after she'd apologized about last night. Even when she'd all but admitted how mortified she'd been. He'd warned her, no more *coddling*. If he knew she had pretended to be asleep just to keep from crawling into his sleeping bag and kissing him senseless—what would he have called it then? Insubordination?

She huffed out air, half amused, half exasperated as she went for water for the mules. Whenever Kody acted that tough-guy role, it seemed more like a cover. But for what? Why was he so opposed to teddy bears? Why didn't he believe in the power of love? She intended to find out. But first she had to prove to him that her coddling days were over.

"Okay, Mo." She slapped the sweaty old mule on the rump. "You take a nice nap while I whip this place into shape." She retied the scarf at the back of her neck and set off to the cabin.

Hot, musty air flowed from the open doorway. Inside Kody had already hooked the shutters open and was propping up a window above a bunk bed.

"Fresh air," he mumbled. "The place has been closed all winter." He moved to the window on the left wall.

Becca stepped into the shadowy interior and felt beside the door for a light switch. "Oh." She stifled a squeal and snatched her fingers back from the sticky tickle of cobwebs on rough logs.

No *electricity?* The kerosene lamp hanging from the middle of the low ceiling confirmed her worst fears. A propane stove sat in one corner and a wood-burning stove stood on the left.

She hadn't expected the cabin to be quite so... primitive. Or so small. To the right, a sink leaned into a stand of shelves filled with cooking utensils and canned goods. Two bunk beds stood against opposite walls, and a long table sat smack in the middle of the room.

"No chairs?"

"Stools. Under the table."

"Only four beds?"

"Most everybody sleeps outside unless it gets too cold. Or we get a real gully-washer." Kody propped up the window at the sink, took two steps and stopped beside the table.

"You can get busy in here while I carry stuff in from the wagon." He dragged a handkerchief from his jeans pocket, swiped his neck, then stood refolding the large white square.

In the close confines of the cabin, he reminded her of a big bear. Except that a bear simply would have lumbered forward and scared her out of his way. Kody fidgeted.

That made her want to smile... and to stay planted right where she was until he had to deal with her. But she knew he'd probably just start issuing orders again.

"Okay, Kody, I'll need a couple of buckets of water, some rags... and a broom." Slowly she moved out of his way. The relief on his face succeeded in making her grin.

Three long strides carried him to the doorway. "There's a spring across the clearing. I'll bring water. If you want it hot, you'll have to heat it. I'll show you how to light the stove." Holding his hat in place, he ducked outside.

"Kody, dinner—I mean, supper—will be ready in two hours. I'll set the table to eat in here."

He paused. Turned back to consider her. "Okay. While you're at it, fix up one of the beds. You'll be sleeping in here, too."

Kody had to stop treating Becca as if she were the enemy. He splashed rainwater onto his face, slapped a handful on the back of his neck, and combed wet fingers through his hair. Grabbing a square of old terrycloth towel from the nail on the side of the cabin, he gave himself a punishing rub.

Guilt was a hell of an emotion. Made him act worse than a grizzly. Ordering Becca around, telling her how to clean, where to sleep. Letting Griswold think she was his fiancée.

Or was he really just fighting anger because he couldn't keep her out of his mind?

In the fading light, he contemplated his hat hanging on another nail and decided it wouldn't do for Becca's indoor supper. Moving reluctantly to the doorway, he stopped to look in.

She stood at the stove stirring something in a pan. Such a little bit of a woman, yet she seemed to fit the small cabin perfectly. He couldn't help but notice her fresh white blouse tucked neatly into sleek-fitting jeans and the bright green scarf holding back the golden mane of her brushed hair.

Close observations like those were what got him into trouble. For that matter, he needed to avoid closeness of all kinds. Eating inside with her would be his one concession, his penance for treating her so badly. For the duration of one meal, he'd make an effort to be...nice.

He stepped into the cabin and rasped uneasiness from his throat. Becca turned, her face brightening with a smile that tucked in the dimple he'd tried so hard to forget. "Kody."

His name was all she said, yet that soft, corduroy voice made him feel as if she were welcoming someone special. Damn. Not a good start.

"Come sit down. Everything's ready."

Everything but him. Tonight the cabin felt cool and fresh. The crisp, clean scent of soap lingered in corners where the spicy aroma of meat and onions hadn't yet reached. Above the table, the kerosene lamp cast an amber glow over the flatware and tin plates she'd arranged on paper towels... with more towels, folded like napkins, at the side. In the center, a rainbow of wildflowers overflowed a bowl.

Everywhere, he found traces of Becca. They drew him in. He crossed the uneven plank floor, scanning the outer reaches of the light. On the top bunk next to the far window, her sleeping bag lay smoothed out and waiting. Quickly he pulled his gaze back to the table and lowered himself onto a stool.

Becca set a bowl of meat in front of him. "Go ahead. Help yourself."

She moved back to the stove. "I hope you like stir-fry because the vegetables I brought needed to be used."

Returning, she brought a steaming bowl, then turned away again. "I'm trying to figure out how we can have fresh vegetables and fruit when we come up with the boys because—"

"Becca, will you *sit*. You're making me nervous."

She was nervous. He could tell. She set the coffeepot on the table and slid onto the opposite stool. Just as quickly, she was up again.

"I forgot bread." Returning with a plate stacked high, she sat down. Crumbs speckled the table, and she brushed them into a pile, then swept them into her hand.

"Don't even think of getting up again. Just put the crumbs on the floor."

Her eyebrows arched, and the flash in her eyes told him he'd just expressed a very bad idea.

Damn. He was off to a poor start. Maybe he'd just plain forgotten how to be nice. Maybe he'd never known.

"Look, Becca, I'm sorry." For interrupting her. For bossing her around. For wanting to stay here with her inside this warm cocoon she'd created. All night.

"Don't worry about feeding the boys. Trail grub will probably be better than what they're used to anyhow. Besides, it's part of the cowhand experience."

She spooned vegetables onto her plate, then handed him the bowl. "Tell me what they are used to."

She wouldn't be coming along on The Journey, so there wasn't any reason for her to know. But he'd vowed to spend this time with her . . . *nicely*.

He tried a bite of the stir-fry. "Not bad for vegetables. I doubt any of them have ever eaten *this*."

"Why?"

She still hadn't figured it out, still didn't understand the distance between their worlds.

"Look, Becca, these are kids of mixed blood. Their skins range from adobe to sandstone . . . with every variation in between."

He could almost feel her trace his skin, gauging, for the first time, the color of his forearms and the bare patch in the open V of his shirt. Her gaze dropped to her plate where her food remained untouched.

When she finally looked up, there were questions in her eyes. Questions about him.

Questions he needed to answer. "These boys' parents might be a Martinez and a Yazzi." *Or a Kawanyuma and a Sanville—why didn't he just say it?* "They don't grow up in normal families like you did. They're rejected everywhere they turn." *Just as he'd been rejected—by his mother's clan. By his father's wealthy East Coast parents.*

Becca sighed. "Why does prejudice thrive whenever people who are different try to live together?"

Her sympathy threatened to undo him. But she couldn't really understand. "These kids don't have a place to belong...not like you did as a kid." *Not like you do now.* "Unless someone intervenes."

"Why are you trying to intervene?"

He'd started this, and she was going to make him finish. He shrugged. "My father left me the ranch."

"Owning a ranch isn't a reason, Kody. Did your father want you to do this?"

He all but snorted. "My father would turn in his grave if he saw the kids from The Journey who'll be working on the Sanville Star." Reynard Sanville had probably already done a couple of twists since Kody had changed the name and the brand.

He needed some coffee. Reaching for the pot, he poured them each a cup.

Becca retrieved hers and regarded him over the rim. "And your mother?"

Kody almost dropped his own cup. She was forcing him to tell it all.

"It wasn't her idea, but she approves of The Journey."

Becca's eyes widened. "She's still alive?"

He nodded slowly. It was too late to turn back now. "She lives with her people, in Arizona. The Bear Clan. On the Hopi reservation."

He waited for the familiar reaction, the slow understanding, the shock, before her gaze slid away to something inconsequential while she tried to find the politically correct words to say.

But her fingers crept to the small charm on the chain around her neck, the knot of gold he'd seen her touch sometimes when she looked sad.

"Then you can visit her."

This wasn't what he'd expected—these words that wavered between wistfulness and anger, the same sadness in her eyes.

"I see her at least once a year."

He stood, scraping the stool backward on the uneven floor. He had to choose—stay with her here in this accepting haven and become more captured in this swirl of unexplored feelings ... or flee to the safety of the night.

But then, there really wasn't a choice, was there?

"I've had enough, Becca. It's been a hard day. I'll help you clean up. Then I need to get out of here and get some sleep."

She stood abruptly, knocking the stool over behind her. "No, this is my job. You won't be helping when the boys are here." Leaving the stool where it lay, she carried their dishes to the sink. "Just bring me a bucket of fresh water."

Too many feelings were filling the cabin...like smoke rising from a carefully banked fire. He needed to escape, but now that she was sending him away, he didn't want to go.

Reluctantly, he strode from the cabin, slowing as he crossed the moonlit clearing to the spring. Looking back, he saw her silhouetted in the cabin doorway, leaning against one side, arms wrapped around her midriff. She was watching him.

His resolve faltered. He scooped up a bucketful of water and headed back, his pace increasing with each stride.

Then Becca turned and went back inside.

Chapter Eight

Cool air whispered through the screened cabin window, telling the secrets of the night. Becca drew the sleeping bag closer, not because she was cold...or even afraid. The simple truth was she wanted to be in Kody's arms.

She sighed—a sad-hearted way of letting go. Lying alone in a dark mountain cabin on a sagging bunk bed mattress, staring out at millions of faraway stars, had to be about the loneliest feeling in the whole world. Especially when the man who caused her longing wanted nothing to do with her.

But even a haunting by one of Kody's skinwalkers wouldn't send her running to him tonight.

She watched the clouds, washed in the glow of Kody's thunder moon, drift across the framed piece of sky. Where had he settled his sleeping bag tonight? Was he watching the same whitewashed clouds? What was he thinking?

Not of her. He'd brought the bucket of water and hurried off after supper as if he couldn't get away from her fast enough. Because she'd asked too many questions. Because he'd revealed too much of himself.

She'd seen the young Kody in his face, the features of a white child carved in bronze. She'd seen his empathy for the boys—understanding that could only have been hard-earned.

Becca turned away from the window. Listening to the high-pitched *weet, weet, weet* of a cricket above the steady ripple of the creek, she tried to put Kody out of her mind. Whatever he had suffered, he'd buried deeper than she knew how to reach. Maybe he shared it with no one. Certainly, not with a *coddled* Covington woman. He'd made that clear.

He was causing too many unwanted reactions... feelings she couldn't blame on high altitude or overwrought hormones or curiosity anymore. She was beginning to care for him.

Somewhere in the distance, the hollow, sad call of a dove mingled with the sadness in her heart. A dove? She listened more carefully to the throaty notes curling along the breeze like strands of silver, weaving themselves into a quiet melody.

This wasn't a dove. It sounded like a flute...breathing notes so soft they seemed wrapped in velvet. They rode the wind with a haunting melody full of longing.

She remembered the slender wooden instrument that had hung from Kody's saddlebag. Somewhere out there in the moonstruck night, he was making music.

Becca rolled off the side of the bed and dropped to the cold floor, then searched on the lower bunk for her clothes. Slipping them on, she shoved into her boots and made her way through the moonlit cabin.

Outside, the coals of a fire drew her gaze. Nearby, Kody's horse stood like a golden statue next to the mahogany figures of the mules. But there was no sign of Kody.

The full moon bathed the ground in light, making it easy for her to follow the lure of the music. She slipped through a narrow opening in the tangle of bushes along the river. That was when she saw him.

Like a magnificent statue, he stood on a flat rock at the edge of the water. Moonlight edged him with diamond dust, casting the planes of his face into shades of luster and shadow like a rough-hewn Rodin. His ebony hair was streaked with moonlight, and it brushed the broad shoulders of his denim jacket.

His eyes were closed, as if he were lost in the sounds that flowed from the instrument he held to his mouth. His fingers moved along the length of the burnished wood, making music that was bittersweet and full of yearning.

Becca forgot to breathe. He was so beautiful. Like a forest god or a lost spirit. His melancholy seemed to whisper from somewhere deep inside, giving voice to the anguish she'd sensed in him.

His music touched her own sadness, and she wondered if he was grieving. She longed to hold him, to find comfort in comforting him. But his music faltered and her heart nearly stopped. She didn't want him to find her here.

Please, don't stop. She waited unmoving, willing him to go on.

The music changed, flowed low and haunting, wrapped around her like a bewitching wind spirit, coiled through her like a shaman's potion. It moved over her and through her, and each note became a caress—tracing her face, touching her skin—until she felt liquid and wanting. Kody's song was turning her inside out with longing.

Was it possible for a man to make love with his music?

No. The passion she heard was only what she wanted to hear. With the last of her willpower, she turned to leave.

Suddenly the night fell silent save for the rush of the river.

"Becca?"

Kody knew she was here.

"Don't go." His voice was deep and compelling.

Any answer she might have given caught in her throat. She waited, breathless and dazed, as if she were watching a dream unfold. He stepped from the rock and glided through the silvery darkness across the space between them. For an eternity, he stood before her, searching her face.

She didn't know if she uttered the soft plea that ached in her throat, but suddenly he pulled her to him, and she felt the warm fullness of his lips. His mouth closed over hers, firm and hungry, and his fingers stole through her loose hair. Yet he held back as if waiting for an answer.

The only answer she knew was to kiss him back, to slide her hands into the thick mane of his hair and arch against the solidity of his body. He made starfire burst inside her, made moonglow curl through her limbs until she felt weak with desire and heat.

His kiss deepened, his mouth opening to claim more of her, and she answered with urgency, tasting his moist, masculine flavor. She met his questing thrusts with her own and felt the moan that escaped from his throat.

His hands slipped under her jacket, and she cried out, soft and hoarse. Every inch of her body came alive to his touch. He cupped her breast, calling the sound from her again. His caress was so gentle, so inflaming, she knew she would burst into a shimmering cloud of desire if he didn't make love to her right then. There, on the forest floor. In the light of the thunder moon.

Murmuring with need and hunger, she slid her fingers to his shirtfront, struggled with the buttons, wanting to feel the heat of his bronze skin against hers.

But suddenly his hands no longer caressed her. Easing from the kiss, he captured her fingers against his chest and held her still.

She rose on tiptoe to lure him back, and he leaned to capture her lower lip again in urgent, nipping kisses. Then with a moan, he pulled away, pressed her curled fingers to his mouth, raised black lashes to reveal eyes full of pain.

"I'm sorry, Becca." His voice was gentle. Hollow. And sad.

"Kody—?"

Still holding her wrists like handcuffs, he stepped back. "Go back to the cabin. Get some sleep. We'll leave at first light."

"No. Please. Why?"

"Just go, Becca." This time his words were hoarse with anger. "I'll watch to see you get back okay."

Kody…? Her heart cried a thousand questions as she stumbled back to the cabin, but she knew he wouldn't answer. Just as she knew it would do no good to try to sleep. She couldn't deny it any longer. She cared for Kody. And *he* wanted *her.*

But he'd rejected her again.

* * *

Kody let his horse prance ahead of the wagon, feeling the animal's agitation as sharply as his own. "As soon as we get there, drive the wagon to the barn. I'll take care of the mules. You get supper started."

"Right." Becca gave him a sharp salute.

Coming from one of the boys, such impudence probably would have amused Kody. Coming from Becca, it just caused another surge of guilt. He gave his horse freedom to trot farther ahead, more anxious than ever to be back at the ranch. Away from Becca.

He had sure earned his nickname on this trip, because he'd been a bear the whole damn time. But what else could he do? He wanted this woman in a way no man should—unless he intended to make her his wife.

But his intentions for Becca were far from honorable. He was going to send her away—to get her out of his life—before he made a mistake they would both regret. He'd take her to Albuquerque first thing in the morning. He'd tell her after supper tonight.

Tugging his horse's reins, he circled back to the wagon. "Give those mules a little leather there. We're not going to a picnic. You're too easy on them."

If there was even an ounce of truth in what he said, he might have been able to excuse his behavior. But Becca handled the mules as well as any of his cowhands. She'd done a fine job the whole trip. And she hadn't complained, hadn't uttered one word on which he could blame his surliness. There was only that brief flash in her eyes. Anger? Defiance? Hurt? A look he wasn't ready to understand.

Damn. The last thing he wanted was to hurt her. But he should have thought of that before he took her into his arms. Before he kissed her so completely.

The memory of the passion that had erupted between them sent him galloping away, putting Becca and the last turn in the trail as far behind as possible.

At the foot of the long slope, the Sanville Star spread out before him, horse barn and windmill, old-fashioned bunkhouse, the chicken coop J.S. had added and, at the center, the big, two-story log mansion rising solid and substantial.

A handsome collection of buildings. The sight filled him with deep anticipation. Someday they would be his home, in his name, his place to belong. As soon as his attorney helped him break the trust contained in his father's will.

Below, a screen door slammed and a short, wiry figure shuffled across the front porch. A white apron covered the man from chest to knees. There was no mistaking the stooped shoulders and bowed legs. *What the devil was J.S. doing back?*

Kody spurred his horse down the trail at a gallop, pulling to a dust-boiling stop at the bottom porch step.

"What the *hell* are you doing here? Why aren't you in the hospital? Or home with Callie?" He studied the old man's face anxiously.

J.S. squinted, hiding his pupils behind short white lashes. "Darned if you don't look mad enough to swallow a horned toad backward. Is that any kind of a way to greet an old friend? 'Specially one who's had a brandin' iron run straight through his veins."

In an instant, Kody was off his horse. He stopped halfway up the stairs, suddenly uncertain what to do. He loved this old coot, and J.S. looked far from being well.

"Damn it, you should be in bed." He gave in to his feelings then, let them carry him up the last steps to give the lean old man a hug. For a moment, Kody felt J.S.'s tight grip on his shoulders. Then he pushed Kody away.

"Horse patooty! Doc had me on my feet the first day. And Callie kicked me clean out of the pueblo. Said I was driving her crazy. Besides, had to come see fer myself the pretty little filly I hear you brought home to cook."

The wagon rumbled round the turn, and J.S.'s face screwed into another squint. "She drives mules, too?"

"She does all right." Kody chose his words cautiously. If J.S. got a whiff of what Kody was feeling for Becca, the old man would never let him hear the last of it.

"That's not what I heard."

Kody swung around. "What *did* you hear?"

"Now, don't start screechin' like a plucked jaybird."

Damn again. Kody could tell from the twinkle in J.S.'s eyes that he was baiting Kody already. What could the men possibly have told him?

"She's drivin' them mules like their tails was afire. Head her over this way, Kody, so's I can make her acquaintance."

Kody followed the old man's orders, waving Becca toward the house.

She guided the mules to a stop at the bottom of the steps like a boat slipping up to a pier. Jumping down, she offered each animal a lump of sugar from her pocket.

"Becca, there's someone wants to meet you."

Watching her climb the steps, he was shocked to see how much she'd changed in the short time she'd been here. Her boots were scuffed and dusty, doomed never to know white again. A hole gaped in the knee of her tight-fitting jeans, and her aqua shirt, sleeves rolled to her elbows, tails tied at her midriff, bore streaks of darker blue-green where the dampness of her skin had soaked through.

She snatched off her once-white hat to rub a forearm across her forehead, brushing back the damp coils of hair that had escaped her braid. Her skin glowed a golden tan except for the creamy white band just below her hairline. She looked like an overheated, hard-working cowgirl. She looked positively beautiful.

"J.S., meet Becca Covington."

J.S. stepped forward and stuck out his hand. "Jedidiah Solomon Jaramillo, ma'am. Pleased to meetcha."

In spite of the dimple that dented Becca's cheek, Kody had to drag his gaze away to stare at his cook. *"Jedidiah Solomon?"*

J.S. just ignored him. "'Course, no cowpoke in his right mind would go by a moniker like that. Folks 'round here call me J.S. My grandson says it's short for Jinjer Snap since I'm the cooky. I figure that's as good a name as any."

"Pleased to meet you, Mr. Jaramillo. I've been trying to fill your shoes—maybe I should say your pots—while you were gone."

She kept hold of J.S.'s hand, and Kody saw her examine the old man's face with concern.

"I hope you're better now."

"Takes more'n a little heart hiccup to keep me down, young lady, but you call me J.S. or not at all, understand?"

"You got it, J.S." Becca grinned.

Kody recognized the twist in his chest for what it was. Becca didn't smile when *he* issued orders.

He thumped down the porch steps. "I'll drive the wagon around back. Becca, you get cleaned up and give J.S. a hand in the kitchen."

Remembering his resolve, he stopped at the bottom of the stairs. "I want to talk to you after supper."

"Hate to postpone your chance to gussy up, Miz Becca, but I need to talk to Kody. Right now." He aimed two fingers straight at Kody. "So if you wouldn't mind—"

"Of course not." She brushed by Kody and pulled up into the wagon seat, then turned to look back. "I'll be on the back porch after supper...if you want to talk." He watched the wagon roll away and suddenly felt tired. Small wonder, after two nights of little sleep... and *big* frustrations. He had to send Becca away tomorrow. Slowly he climbed the porch steps, one heavy foot after another.

But J.S. was offering no sympathy. "Jest what is it you're fixin' to talk to her about after supper?" Mischief sparkled in his dark eyes. "An' wouldn't you be better off *talking* someplace real private?"

"I'm going to fire her." The words came out more blunt than Kody meant, but he wanted to squelch J.S.'s needling.

"Since when you been studying up to be a half-wit?"

"I don't need her. Especially now that you're back. But I wasn't going to keep her, anyhow. I'm not going to *use* her, J.S. I'll find another way to keep the ranch."

"Well, I'll be damned. The men was right. She's as purty as a little jersey heifer in a flower bed. And you're flat in love."

J.S.'s words hit like a charging bull. *Love?* Love had nothing to do with his reactions to Becca. What he felt for her was desire. Not exactly the everyday, garden variety...more like Sanville passions run rampant. But nothing more.

"And *you,* old man, must be on some pretty heavy meds."

"Yep," J.S. answered quietly.

Kody felt like that bull had turned right around and hit him again. Real hard. "Then what the—?"

"Doc told me I could come back if I promised to take it easy. I can help in the kitchen like I been helpin' Ike while you was gone. I can spend some time with the boys. But I can't go on The Journey."

"Then I'll hire another cook. I'll start calling around right away." Kody turned to the kitchen door.

"You can't fire her, Kody. You need her."

When J.S. talked in that deep, certain voice, Kody knew he'd better pay attention. "Need her? Camp cooks aren't that hard to come by, you know that."

"Good ones are . . . and *you* know *that.* The men tell me she's good *and* a hard worker. I hear tell she's got the education to deal with the boys, too."

"I won't use her to keep the ranch."

"Then don't. Tell the attorney the truth if that's what you gotta do, but don't send her away jest 'cause you're afraid of gettin' branded."

"You know I'll never—"

The screen door swung open, and Becca stepped out. "Do the vegetables in the sink need cleaning for tonight, J.S.?"

"You got it, Becca. I'll be right in." He winked.

The screen door had barely closed before he turned back to Kody. "Listen, son, only a fool argues with a skunk . . . or a camp cook. Only a fool would send that woman away."

Kody grabbed his hat and jammed his fingers through his hair. He paced the length of the porch and stopped at the far end to glare up at the mountains. The Journey had to be a success, and he knew J.S. was right. Becca would be good.

He glanced back at the old man, who'd settled into the porch rocker. Kody had never known J.S. to sit in that chair. Damn it, the man wasn't well.

Stomping back, he glared down at J.S. "All right. She stays until the doctor says you're fit. Then she goes."

"I know'd you had more under that hat than hair." A grin spread across J.S.'s face, but the old man's smile didn't hide the dark circles under his eyes or improve the color of his sallow skin.

They were enough to convince Kody he'd made the right decision. He'd just have to make a few changes in the way things ran around here. First he'd call Griswold and let him know Becca was only hired help. Then he'd move J.S. up from the bunkhouse.

He didn't have to know he'd be the resident chaperon.

J.S. pushed up from the rocker. "Guess I better get in there an' help the new cook." He paused at the front door. "Forgot to tell you, Kody. Callie said, when you go to the pueblo to get Tom, bring Becca along."

"*Why?*" But J.S. had already disappeared into the ranch house. For once Kody was glad his cook came down with bouts of selective deafness. But why did Callie want Becca to come to the pueblo? Callie had always been a good friend. Surely she wasn't jealous.

Surely she wouldn't tell Becca the terms of his father's will.

Becca saw the sign through the open window of the pickup. Three more miles to the pueblo.

"Thank goodness we're almost there. Do they make these trucks specially for cowboys?"

"What do you mean?" Kody kept his eyes on the road.

It was possibly the longest sentence he'd spoken to her since they'd come back from the mountains two days ago.

"I mean, do they leave the seat springs and shocks out on purpose? Or is it just a guy thing to always want to feel like you're riding a horse?" And why did Kody drive such a junker when the rest of the ranch was so modern?

Kody actually turned to look at her. A trace of humor hitched up one brow. "It's a budget thing. The truck was cheap...and it runs."

Becca's heart flickered with hope. Could he possibly be loosening up? She'd been waiting two whole days. After that shattering kiss, she'd been sure he was going to send her away. But she'd known the minute she met J.S. that he wasn't ready to take over his old job.

So Kody had decided to keep her. And to stay as far away from her as he could get.

But today he'd asked her to ride with him to the pueblo, and now he'd almost smiled. Maybe there was still hope.

Ahead, she saw a cluster of small, square homes scattered among cottonwood trees around a dusty clearing.

"I thought this was a pueblo."

"It is. The original mud houses are down by the creek. Most of the younger people live here."

They pulled into the clearing, and Kody beeped the horn. The half-dozen adults at the far end turned and waved. From behind several of the houses, a flock of smaller figures scrambled into sight, and several more dashed from a nearby hillside.

Children! They ran toward the truck chanting, "Ko-dy, Ko-dy."

Pulling to a stop, Kody launched himself out the door.

Becca climbed out the other side and held back to watch.

The children descended on him in a gang, and Kody bent to meet them. He hugged small bodies and rumpled shiny black hair. He patted shoulders and checked for lost teeth, then scooped up a tiny wide-eyed toddler with straight dark hair and a round, smiling face. He lifted her to his hip and kissed her on the nose.

Beaming, she patted his cheeks. "Kooo-deee," she cooed.

"Sweet little dove." He swung the little girl high above his head, then swooped her back to earth, laughing at her cascade of giggles.

Becca's heart all but melted. The children seemed to adore Kody, and he obviously cared for them.

Why had he never married? Why didn't he have children of his own?

Several of the children grabbed Kody by the arm and tugged, taking up a new chant. "Base—*ball*, base—*ball*."

Becca was surprised that he glanced back at her. She shrugged. "Hey, I'm not going anywhere till the boss does."

Another smile almost broke through his reserve. He took a quick survey of the whole area before he turned. "Okay, kids, one inning."

They followed him like a swarm of gnats to the middle of the clearing where he began dividing them into teams.

"Tom! We need one more person." He beckoned to a lanky-limbed boy slumped against the side of an old blue-and-white Chevrolet parked near one of the houses.

The boy wore baggy, knee-length shorts and an oversized T-shirt. He couldn't have been more than eleven or twelve, but his face was clenched in the angry pout of a teenager.

Tom Walker, Becca concluded, the boy they'd come to take back for The Journey.

Instead of joining the game, the boy shifted his weight from one foot to the other and stared in the opposite direction.

In the clearing, Kody accepting a proffered bat and whacked it on the heel of his boot. "Tom, we need you on our team."

Scornfully the boy pushed away from the car and slouched toward them, kicking a rock ahead of him. For some reason, his manner reminded Becca of Kody.

"I hope you have success with Tom on The Journey."

Startled, Becca turned. "Callie!" She smiled. "I thought that was the boy we'd come to pick up."

The tall, bronze-skinned woman barely returned her smile. "J.S. thinks Kody can get to him. I guess Kody thinks you can, too."

Becca had forgotten how exotically lovely Callie was, even in black jeans and a bright red blouse.

"J.S. and Kody seem pretty close."

"They are." Callie turned her attention to Kody.

Becca didn't remember Callie being so unfriendly, but the affection in her eyes as she watched Kody told Becca why. Understanding shot through her with pure jealousy.

Kody looked up from dividing the kids and caught sight of Callie. He waved and started toward them, but one of the children grabbed his arm. Kneeling, he talked with the child, glancing back more than once, worry written across his face. When he finally caught Callie's eye, he frowned.

What was going on? Becca looked back at Callie in time to see disappointment touch her face. Her chin rose and she held Kody's gaze hard until his face slowly relaxed.

Becca's spirits dipped. This must be what it felt like to be an outsider—to be excluded from the meanings that passed between people who were close. She glanced with empathy at the boy called Tom Walker. He stood apart from the other children, who were wrestling and laughing on the field. No wonder he looked angry. And hurt.

"Okay, Tom. You pitch. Remember what I showed you last time." Kody followed a pint-sized kid to home plate and helped him hold a very big bat.

Whatever had passed between Kody and Callie must have satisfied him, because the children held his attention now.

"He's so good with children," Callie murmured.

The wistfulness in Callie's voice made her feelings clear. Suddenly Becca remembered Callie's radiance when she'd walked with Kody in Trey's wedding. The memory made her earlier hope wither.

"You're in love with him, aren't you."

For a moment, Callie's dark eyes searched hers. Then she turned sharply back to the game. "What a woman feels for Kody is of no importance."

What did she mean? Was Callie trying to warn her off?

Callie continued to stare out at the game. Tom pitched the ball, and Kody helped the child swing. A loud crack signaled a hit, and shouts filled the air. Turning the tyke by the shoulders, Kody scooted him in the direction of the rock they'd designated as first base.

"Great pitch, Tom," Kody hollered. "You've been practicing."

"You *hit* it," the boy snarled back. "You're not supposed to be able to hit it."

"But you made one little guy feel pretty tough."

Suddenly Callie whirled back to Becca. "You see how good he is with kids, how much love he has? He should have children of his own." Her voice trembled with anguish.

"Why doesn't he, Callie? Why isn't Kody married?"

For an instant, Becca saw pain in Callie's eyes.

"Kody will never take a woman. He will never repeat the sins of his father."

Then she turned and strode away. Leaving Becca with a sense of foreboding. Taking the last of her hope.

Chapter Nine

The truck jounced along the dirt road. Becca braced her boots against the threadbare floor mat and glanced at the taciturn males on either side—Kody squinting straight ahead, Tom staring out the side window.

Times like this, she could sympathize with a rodeo bull. Poor beast, held captive inside that narrow wooden chute just like she was trapped between these two obstinate males. Except that Tom slouched as far away from her as he could get, and Kody leaned the other direction, resting his bare forearm on the open window frame.

"Tom, I'll bet you're looking forward to driving Kody's cattle."

"No." He hung his skinny little arm farther out the window. The wind whipped his chin-length black hair.

No mistaking this boy's body language. He was on the lookout for his first chance to escape. But she knew better than to be put off.

"Callie said you were a fast learner. We'll need cowhands like that on The Journey."

"Callie don't know me," Tom grumbled.

"Callie told me you'd be one of my best hands." Kody's casual tone implied Tom's success was just a matter of time.

"Callie don't know nothin'." Tom glared at them defiantly, then jerked back to the window.

Becca inhaled slowly. Tom was going to need a lot of patience. On the other hand—her left, to be exact—Kody wasn't any better. He'd retreated into his eyes-forward, hat-low posture—a man who didn't want to be messed with.

But he had brought her along. He *had* almost smiled.

And what Callie had said made Becca wonder. Maybe the reason Kody rejected her wasn't because she was a "soft city woman." Not if he'd turned away from Callie, too.

Kody won't repeat his father's mistakes. If only Becca knew what Callie had meant.

"Kody, Callie said—"

His head snapped around. "*What* did Callie tell you?"

The question hovered between them, a demand he'd barely managed to soften with a shade of appeal. It told her so much more than Callie had...that there were things Kody didn't want Becca to know, places in his heart he didn't want her to see.

"She said...you were good with kids."

The truck gears grated as he shifted for an incline, and the protest almost seemed to come from within him.

Why wouldn't Kody marry? What were his father's mistakes that kept him from loving a woman? From giving his heart to a family?

He turned to her again, as if he were trying to read her face. "Did Callie talk about the Sanville Star?"

"We talked mostly about the kids."

Some of the stiffness eased from his shoulders, and he turned back to the road.

She studied the lines etched in his angular face and wondered what troubles had worn them there. Were there problems with the ranch?

Why would he drive an old junker of a truck? Why would he keep such a small crew of cowhands? A mule-drawn chuck wagon had to be less expensive to operate, and at-risk boys didn't have to be paid for a cattle drive.

Maybe the elder Sanville's mistakes meant leaving his son a ranch with no money to run it.

Was Kody rejecting her because she came from money?

They passed through the Sanville Star entrance and sped down the juniper-lined road to the ranch. A van and a station wagon sat parked in front of the house.

Kody pulled the truck to a stop next to the two vehicles. "Looks like the rest of the new hands have arrived. Grab your stuff from the back, Tom. I'll show you the bunkhouse. Becca, there'll be eleven for lunch." He disappeared out the driver's-side door.

Tom made his escape from the other door, leaving Becca sitting alone in the middle of the cab.

"We'll be ready," she murmured, already missing Kody's solid presence and the warm, masculine scents of outdoors and play. Knowing she shouldn't be missing them at all.

Sliding out, she watched the two males retrieve Tom's belongings and head away. Kody's stride was longer than the boy's, but Tom didn't try to catch up. Backpack slung low on one shoulder, he hid his downcast face behind blunt-cut black hair, except when he stole furtive glances at the ranch.

Somehow she knew these two were more alike than different. Too stubborn for their own good. Too proud.

Was Kody too proud to ask for help with the ranch?

The two of them swung around the corner of the house, and for a moment, Kody looked back. His gaze sought hers—the awareness made her heart stumble. Then he tugged down his hat and followed Tom out of sight.

Maybe she shouldn't give up hope, after all.

Hurrying up the front porch steps, she entered the welcoming adobe foyer and noticed five clean cowboy hats hanging on the side wall. At the kitchen door, she stopped, taking in the bright tiles and hanging *ristra* of chilies with an unexpected sense of homecoming.

J.S. jacked his short frame from a four-legged stool and set a bowl on the counter. "Well, looka here, Miss Becca, you caught me sittin' on my end gate." He grinned broadly. "Things been quieter 'n a hole in the ground 'round here. Where's the boss 'n' all them boys?"

J.S. made her smile even when she didn't feel like it. She grabbed an apron from a peg. "They're down at the bunkhouse. Be up for lunch soon. What needs to be done?"

J.S. filled her in on the menu, and she went to work. Returning from setting the dining room table, she lifted the lid from the pot on the stove and stole a taste.

"Now, *git* outta there!"

She laughed, sidestepping J.S.'s flicking towel. "This is *wonderful*. What is it?"

"Stew. Flavored with sunflower seeds and cornmeal. From an old Hopi recipe—from Kody's mama."

Becca replaced the lid and turned to the fresh loaf of bread on the butcher-block island. "Tell me about Kody's mama."

J.S. handed her a knife. "Never met her, but Kody says she was a purty one. They called her Red Bird cause of the music she made and how light she moved."

"What about his father?"

J.S. stacked the sliced bread on a plate and shuffled off to the dining room. Returning, he squinted one eye and scratched behind an ear.

"Miss Becca, most men's like bob wire, I reckon. They all have their good points. But Reynard Sanville, well, Kody's mama musta loved him, but they say you can't hitch up a horse with a coyote."

Becca searched J.S.'s face. "I don't understand."

"Means a fox can't hitch up with a red bird and expect his cub not to have feathers." J.S. slammed a drawer and stomped out of the kitchen with another plate of bread.

Kody was a child of two different cultures—she'd understood that at the cabin. But what was it like to be a fox cub with feathers? Or a bird that couldn't fly?

Becca's fingers found the knot of gold wire hanging from the chain around her neck. How different was Kody from her, really? Becca Covington, daughter of an unemotional, by-the-books, money-making father... and a mother who had overflowed with love and generosity.

What kind of cub did that make her? An unfortunate combination of qualities, she was afraid. Kind of like a puppy with porcupine quills. Too quick to accept, too eager to give. The baby Covington everyone thought still needed paper training. But she was like her father, too— unwilling to forgive...even though his silence about her mother's imminent death had been to protect her. Afraid to take risks, like moving away from Vermont and the family security. Too inflexible to—

"A person oughta be *sure* he can live with the *differences,* Miss Becca." J.S. still sounded angry on his return from the dining room. " 'Specially when it comes to gettin' married."

Married? Oh, God.

Shock flooded through her on a wave of stunning guilt. She was practically a married woman, but she'd forgotten all about her postponed wedding. She hadn't thought about Allen since she'd come here. Not even once.

Five adolescent boys piling into a ranch house for grub should have been like a carload of clowns spilling into the center ring of a circus. But the dining room sounded more like a funeral home—only with less talk.

Becca leaned against the side of the kitchen doorway and watched the boys file in ahead of Kody in stony silence. Ed, Tully and Ike brought up the rear. The boys stopped just inside the archway, each managing to stand apart from the others as if entrenched behind his own invisible wall.

All except Tom. Head up, he glared from one adult to the next, daring them all to send him away.

"Joe, you sit between Ike and Tully. Ricardo, you're on the end. Manny and Carl on this side." Kody assigned the boys their seats, mixing them between the adults. "Tom, you're next to me. Okay, men, Eating Rule Number One?"

Kody's question was met with stony silence.

"Well, hey, boss—" Ike shifted where he stood behind his place at the bench. "No hats in the dining room."

Becca saw the boy named Manny steal a glance into the foyer. A glow of pleasure eased his scowl. That's when she remembered the five new hats hanging there.

So Kody had given one to each of the boys. Protection from the sun was a necessity on the trail, but she knew the gift was more than a practicality. It was a vote of trust, Kody's way of telling the boys they were part of his crew.

And quite an expenditure, Allen would say. *They'll probably sell them when they get home.*

Pushing away from the doorframe, Becca shook her head. Her plan to work with disadvantaged kids was one of the subjects on which she and Allen disagreed.

"Wait, Becca. Please."

Kody's voice was enough to slow her, but the respect in his "magic word" brought her around with raised brows. Surely he knew better than to lay that kind of expectation on these boys. He'd have them jeering at him behind his back before dessert.

"Men, this is Miss Becca." His gaze sought her across the room, surprised her with its warmth. "She's our cook, along with J.S. Now, here's Eating Rule Number Two. Nobody sits till the ladies sit. 'Round here that means Miss Becca."

Surprised, she mustered a weak smile. "Guess I'd better get the grub before these guys fall down from hunger." She beat a hasty retreat, wondering at the protectiveness in Kody's gaze. Knowing she shouldn't be pleased—she should be resisting.

With J.S.'s help, she carried the rest of the food to the table. She slid into her place, avoiding Kody's eyes, unwilling to believe what she'd seen there.

Kody sat down at the head, and the men followed his lead. One by one, the boys slumped onto the benches.

"Okay, men, when we're on the trail, eating will be pretty casual, but a good ranch hand knows how to eat with cows *and* kings. First of all, napkins go on your lap and..."

Kody was giving them a lesson in table manners!

Don't ever try to teach a pig to sing. Becca could hear Allen quoting his favorite argument against working with problem kids. *It wastes your time...and annoys the pig.*

But kids were *people.* She'd always believed that given enough encouragement, everyone had some kind of song to sing.

The thought made her draw in air. She'd completely forgotten that Allen didn't care for music. But the melodies of Kody's songs...and the heat of his kiss...still curled through her memory.

She had to stop comparing the two men. It served absolutely no purpose.

Instead, she made herself focus on the boys. Manny and Carl sat on her side of the table. Both were probably about fourteen, though Manny already nurtured a shadow of dark hair above his lip, while Carl's smooth, dove-brown skin showed no signs of a beard. Tom, Joe and Ricardo sat between the men on the other side like adobe steps, ranging from Tom's ungainly boyishness and Joe's blocky solidness to Ricardo, who was the tallest and lightest of skin. And the most cocky.

What a mixture...a motley crew. She might have grinned if they hadn't all looked old beyond their years—as if they'd never known childhood. They looked angry... and hurt.

There's nothing you can do to change them, Becca. Those kids will break your heart. Allen had said it often enough.

Maybe he was right.

"Hey, Tom, you're supposed to use your fork."

Beside her, Carl waved his fork at Tom like a red flag.

"Don't have to if I don't want to." Tom scooped up a spoonful of stew and slurped it into his mouth.

"Why don'tcha just drink it out of the bowl, Tom Tom." Ricardo winked at Becca. "Like you do at home." He was obviously pleased with his comment.

Tom erupted from the bench and charged the length of the table, fists balled and ready. "Don't call me Tom Tom!"

Instantly, Ricardo was on his feet and looming a full head taller. He sneered down at Tom. "Tom *Tom*."

Tom reared back and swung. His fist smacked smartly against Ricardo's chin. Suddenly the room seemed to explode. Benches scraped backward and men and boys popped up like targets in a shooting gallery.

"Hold on there!" Tully grabbed Tom, but too late. Ricardo's fist connected squarely with Tom's mouth.

"Unh!" Blood welled from the split in Tom's upper lip. His hand flew to the wound, and he ducked his head.

"That's enough!"

Through the commotion, Kody's voice rang firm... and surprisingly free of anger. All eyes turned to where he stood at the head of the table.

"You've exchanged blows. The fight's over. Ricardo, you will call Tom by his given name. You'll also take care of Miss Becca's mules tonight. Tom, you will settle no more disputes with your fists. From now on, at the Sanville Star, anger will be resolved with talk.''

He glanced at Becca, and she saw that rare, dear flash of humor. "Also, after Miss Becca fixes your lip, you will help her clean up the kitchen."

Tom's head jerked up, but he didn't argue.

Suddenly Becca felt laughter building in her chest. What had started out as an impossible situation was beginning to show hope, after all. In more ways than one.

"J.S., if you'll bring dessert while Miss Becca sews Tom up, we'd all appreciate it." Kody sat back down.

Everyone followed his example. Just like that, it was over. But the boys' faces told the story. Kody had meted out perfect punishments. The last thing a Don Juan like Ricardo wanted was to care for a pair of smelly old *mules*. And Tom clearly *hated* the idea of being consigned to the kitchen with a woman.

Yet neither of them protested. They accepted the fairness of his handling. There would be no mocking behind Kody's back from these boys.

Without further instructions, Tom slunk ahead of Becca into the kitchen while the others resettled at the table.

"Okay, Tom, over here to the sink." Running the cold water, she avoided looking at him until he'd swiped at his eyes. Then she made him wash the blood from his hands while she cleaned his face. It wasn't a bad split, just enough to leave a scar worthy of tall tales later. She'd heard her brothers tell them often enough.

But her brothers had never looked as scared as Tom.

"Are you going to sew me?"

Hiding a smile, she rummaged in a drawer for Band-Aids. "I don't think I'll have to. It's a pretty big wound, but I think I can fix it without stitches." Her brothers had always competed over who had the most serious injury.

Quickly she applied disinfectant and butterflied a small Band-Aid across the split, then settled him on the stool with an ice pack.

Tom looked like a kid in a Norman Rockwell painting, knees together, heels of his boots apart, both hands up to hold the pack in place. But for the first time, he sat tall.

Once again Becca had to turn away to hide a smile. She would let him have his fifteen minutes of glory... before she handed him a dish towel.

She helped J.S. carry the last of the dishes to the kitchen and rinsed while he loaded the dishwasher.

He closed the washer door and gave her a wink. "Since you got good help here, reckon I'll go join the others." He shuffled out the back door.

Becca eased the ice pack from Tom's lip. "Let's see how that looks." The bleeding had stopped and the swelling was going down. "Umm, pretty bad. Better sit there a bit longer."

Tom looked pleased.

Steam rose from the sink as she washed the pots and pans and watched the boys through the kitchen window. They had gathered around Kody down by the barn where he was saddling a horse. But none of them stood very near the horse, and their defiance seemed to have diminished.

"I can see Kody and the boys from here."

Tom looked up.

"I thought you boys knew how to ride."

That brought him up off the stool. "What do you see?"

"Looks like Kody's giving lessons. The boys look kind of skittish."

Next thing she knew, Tom stood beside her, stretching over the counter to peer out the window.

"While you're standing here, wipe these pots and pans for me, would you?"

He mustered a rebellious look, but it faded as he watched out the window. Grabbing a pan from the drainer, he swished the towel around the inside.

"Look at them. They're *scared!*" He clanged the pot onto the butcher block behind him and turned back for another. "*I* know how to ride. *I'm* not scared. I'll show them." He dropped the second pot inside the first with a loud clang.

"Tom! I'm not going to fire you even if you dent J.S.'s pots. Now, come here. I want to ask you something."

Warily he turned back to the window.

"Tell me what's wrong with the way Joe's riding?"

He laughed—a sarcastic bark too angry for a boy so young. "He rides like a girl. He's sitting too hard, and he's holding the reins like hair ribbons. The horse can smell his fear."

"Can you teach him better?"

He pulled back from the window and stared at her. "You want *me* to teach them?"

"Do you think you can?"

"I know how to ride." Defiance rang in his words.

"But can you teach them in a way they'll want to learn?"

His round, dark eyes searched hers, then his head dropped. "They're older than me. I'm...not like them. They won't listen to me."

"If you show them your skills, they'll listen. If you give, they'll listen."

For a long time, he stood at the window looking out at the boys, and at the man she couldn't stop watching.

Kody helped Joe climb down from the saddle. Patted him on the shoulder. Rubbed the horse's nose.

What boy wouldn't want to be just like him? What woman wouldn't want—

"I'll try."

Startled, she looked down at the boy who still gazed out the window, his face a mixture of tough street urchin and scared young kid.

Not a lot different from her, really. In Kody's eyes, she was a pampered, city-bred dilettante. But she was really just a not-very-independent, vulnerable woman.

"Good, I'm proud of you. Trying is half the battle." But she had sense enough not to try to hug him...yet. "Learning from failure is the other half."

Tom grabbed the last pot and dusted it with the towel, then deposited it on the butcher block with a gentle thud.

He was learning. But it came to her that Allen would have corrected him for making any noise at all.

"Come on, Miss Becca. Aren't we done yet? Can't we go ride now?"

"Yes." Swiping the sink clean, she wrung out the dishcloth and tossed her apron on a peg. "Get your hat and let's go."

Suddenly she shared Tom's sense of urgency—to get down to the barn, to get involved, to try...again. She'd work with the kids the way they were meant to be treated. She'd work with Kody to help him keep his dream. Because she knew now, with certainty, she didn't want to leave the Sanville Star.

But what would she do if Kody didn't want her to stay? For her, failure would mean learning only one thing: how it felt to have a broken heart.

Chapter Ten

J.S. hung a booted foot on the bottom rail of the corral fence and grinned up at Kody on his horse. "You can stop actin' like a sparrow watching a wormhole now, 'cause here they come."

Any other time, Kody would have at least shot back a friendly oath. But this first afternoon with the boys, when his attention should be strictly on them, he was in no mood to be needled.

Two days since he and Becca had returned from the cabin, and he still couldn't get hold of Griswold . . . two long days of watching over his shoulder to make sure the attorney didn't show up and talk to her. Kody had to be sure Griswold had received his messages, that he knew who she was. More to the point, who she *wasn't*. She was *not* his bride-to-be.

Guiding his horse from the fence, he rejoined the boys in their first plodding ride around the corral. The sight of Becca striding across the ranch yard with Tom in her tracks—and no sign of Griswold—gave him a moment of relief.

Trouble was, Becca stirred too many other reactions, and they lasted far longer than a minute. Just seeing her filled him with a deep, warming pleasure. Becca was taking root at the ranch like a bright cholla flower. More and more she seemed to belong, not just in the kitchen or in the fancy decor of the house, but here, on the land. His land.

It *would* be his. He would find another way.

He watched in amazement as Tom dogged Becca's heels like a faithful dog all the way across the yard, when less than an hour ago he'd incited a small riot in the dining room. Apparently Becca was capable of working small miracles, too.

Kody could use a miracle himself right now...like his own attorney coming up with an idea. And pretty damn soon.

Impatiently he nudged his horse back to the corral fence where Becca and Tom propped a foot up on either side of J.S. The three of them looked like kids peering into a candy store window. He could almost feel how badly they wanted to ride.

Becca tipped her hat back and smiled up at him. "Tom finished KP with flying colors. Mind if we join you?"

Damned if that dimple wasn't enough to soften even the toughest cowboy's heart. Not to mention his *head*.

"*Yes, I mind.* Doc said no riding for J.S., and I don't need a female greenhorn in here. The two of you could help *Tom* onto a horse, though."

Tom kicked the rail, evoking a metallic protest. "I don't need help."

"He's right, boss," J.S. piped up. "Tom can ride." He gave Tom's hat a tug down in front. "Now, don't make a liar out of me, cowboy."

"I can ride, too." Becca's tone rang with barely contained patience as she pushed open the wide metal gate. "Come on, Tom. Let's get us some horses."

Becca was planting herself right in the middle of Kody's program, and somehow he knew it wouldn't do a damn bit of good to tell her no. The thought almost made him grin.

He checked the boys on the other side of the corral. Satisfied they were handling their horses, he rode to the side of the barn.

"Tom, let's see you mount that pinto. Becca, take the Appaloosa. I'll need a demonstration of competence here."

Becca gave Tom a boost, then swung up onto the larger horse with an ease that shouldn't have surprised Kody.

"Okay, you two, down to the end of the corral and back, but take it easy. I don't want the other horses spooked." The words weren't out of Kody's mouth before Tom took off like he was chasing a train.

Young fool! Just had to show off. He'd probably get himself dumped. Kody swung his horse around to give chase.

Just as quickly, Becca danced her horse into his path. "If you go after him, you'll spoil it for him with the other boys." Before he could argue, she trotted away.

Kody stared after her. She was right. If he tried to stop him, Tom would lose face... if he didn't break his fool neck first. Becca was rapidly proving herself in another area... the mysterious art of understanding adolescent boys.

Quickly Kody searched for Tom at the far end of the corral. A trail of dust marked his progress where he urged the pinto in a tight circle as if rounding a barrel. He let out an elated whoop, then, hell-bent for leather, charged back toward Kody. A grin stretched across his face.

This was the first time Kody had ever seen Tom grin. Becca had made that possible.

Just seconds behind, she pulled up in her own churning cloud, smiling as broadly as Tom. "Any other little maneuvers you'd like to see, boss?"

He should have known. She could ride as well as she did everything else he asked of her. If he wasn't careful, he'd be asking her to stay on after J.S. got back on his feet.

"No!"

Tom and Becca's eyebrows rose in unison.

"I mean yes. Give the boys a few more turns around the corral. Then get them down and the horses put up."

In the meantime, he'd just trot himself back to square one, which meant staying away from Becca—as he damned well should have done since the first day she arrived. Kody steered his horse through the gate J.S. held open. "I'm going to try to reach Griswold again." Reining toward the ranch house, he gave the animal freedom to run—away from the sound of Becca's textured voice.

"On your second riding lesson, Tom and I want to..."

Second riding lesson? He jerked the horse around to find the boys gathered in a semicircle in front of Becca and Tom. They looked like a mounted classroom.

Kody's muscles tensed as he watched Becca direct the kids into a line with Tom in the lead. Even though she seemed to have everything under control, he urged his horse back toward the corral. The sight of her teaching the ragtag crew of boys, the way they hung on her words, unknotted some of the tightness in his chest.

Suddenly their pace kicked into a trot. He couldn't be sure who had initiated the change, but sweat slithered down his back. Automatically, he steeled himself. Nudging his mount nearer, he stopped near J.S., beside the still-open gate. He noticed J.S.'s mouth stood open, too.

"That little feller with the bow an' arrow can sure bugger up a cowboy," J.S. murmured, raising his head to squint up at Kody. A grin played at the corners of his mouth. "Thought you was going to call Griswold."

Suddenly the sun felt too warm on Kody's neck. "Half-breeds are immune to Cupid, old man," he growled. J.S. always had a saying to jerk him back to reality. "Keep an eye on things, will you? And close that gate," he hollered back over his shoulder.

Damn. Watching a woman charm rebellious boys was hard on a man, especially a woman like Becca. She was planting herself right in the middle of his dreams, and he didn't seem able to stop her. He didn't want to think about why he wasn't trying.

At the back porch, he swung down from his horse and headed up the steps. Griswold had damn well better be in his office this time.

"Kody!"

He whirled around to find J.S. trudging across the ranch yard waving his hat. "It's Tom. He took off." In the distance, a cloud of dust raced up the trail toward summer pasture.

Kody skimmed back down the steps as another rider charged from behind the barn and thundered after the first. A sheaf of blond hair bounced on her back.

Swearing, he leapt on his horse and urged the animal forward. How could he have left Becca alone with the boys? What could he possibly have been thinking? A hotheaded kid and a soft city woman—two people he cared about more than he let himself admit. Now they were tearing off into a wilderness neither of them knew.

God help him if anything happened to them.

Becca closed the corral gate behind her and led her horse across the enclosed area. She could feel J.S. and the boys watching her, waiting for news...and some kind of a reaction.

"Okay, guys, let's get these horses unsaddled before Kody and Tom get back." A smile was more than she could muster, but she tried at least to project reassurance. The truth was she was terrified, but she couldn't let the boys see that.

She'd made such a mess of things. Kody must have thought she was competing for Miss Rodeo Queen the way she'd been showing off—trying so hard to impress him with her riding skills. She'd let her feelings override good sense. Now Tom might be in real danger.

She helped Carl unfasten the cinch and slide his saddle off, but her heart wasn't in the task. She barely heard J.S.'s grumbling and the sullen silence of the boys.

Kody had been right to order her back to the ranch while he went after Tom. He had every reason to be furious with her. She just wished it didn't hurt so badly.

"Aw right, you young bucks, git over here."

Hauling another saddle off, she looked up to see J.S. herd the four edgy boys into a tight group along the side of the barn. His bowed legs didn't hamper him from pacing back and forth in front of them.

"I think you owe Miss Becca an apology."

"J.S., don't scold them. It was my fault. I shouldn't have given Tom so much leeway."

"Miss Becca, I was watchin', an' Tom was doin' just fine. But *one* of you boys couldn't stand to see him gainin' Miss Becca's favor. I want to know what it was ya done."

The boys shifted, trying to put more space between themselves, but J.S. wasn't backing off.

Becca's spirits dropped another level. Kody would never keep her on at the Sanville Star after she'd created so much conflict. "J.S., really—"

"I got a whole acre of potatoes needs peelin', and I got me four healthy peelers right here 'less somebody decides to come clean."

"All I did was call him a name."

None of the boys looked up. Becca couldn't tell who had made the guilty admission.

"Jest what name did you call him?" J.S. closed in on the group until he stared up at Ricardo.

The boy turned his head to the side. "Half-breed," he muttered. "But it's the truth!"

Half-breed! The word stung Becca like a slap. An outdated word—an epithet from a pulp Western novel—not a name to be hurled like sticks and stones, not at a child.

Tom *was* a child of mixed blood, but surely they all were.

"We're not leavin' till Miss Becca gets an apology."

Ricardo's face tightened with scorn.

Becca put a hand on J.S.'s arm. A confrontation like this could only lead to more trouble. "J.S., I think maybe Ricardo needs to apologize to himself."

The boy's eyes sought hers. He studied her warily.

"I think Ricardo made something bad out of something he and Tom share."

His defiant gaze faltered, and she knew she'd been right. "I think you boys have many things in common. I want to learn about you all...say around the camp fire when we're out on the trail? Ricardo, I'd like to hear from you first."

Ricardo's chin rose, but he and the rest of the boys looked more vulnerable than rebellious as J.S. steered them away, lugging their saddles into the barn.

The sight overwhelmed her. She'd been so naive. *Of course* these boys had suffered. That's why they were here—because they'd been called names, because they'd been mistreated and discriminated against—the same way children back home often were treated...if they were different.

Kody had told her. But somehow it hadn't seemed real. She'd been so caught up in the romance of a cowboy fantasy, the fabrications of a girl, that she hadn't understood. This world—the ranch, the pueblos, the West—was the real world as much as anywhere else. It could be just as harsh. Not the place to chase a young girl's dream.

But somehow she had to convince Kody to keep her at the Sanville Star, to let her continue with the program. If she showed him she finally understood, maybe he would—

"Say there, young lady!"

A shout from outside the corral saved her from having to face what she really wanted from Kody. A man stood at the gate, and he looked vaguely familiar, though she'd never seen so much turquoise and silver. His bolo tie and watchband hung heavy with aqua stones, and his belt buckle shone like a muted green headlight in the middle of his pear-shaped body.

The stranger waved and began mincing his way across the dusty corral.

Of course! She recognized that walk immediately. The suit—Kody's "business appointment"—with the big black car. Watching his fussy approach, she remembered Kody's reaction, his less-than-welcoming smile, the way he'd motioned her away. Kody hadn't liked this man.

He tiptoed over and held out a plump pink hand sporting a large silver ring. He was puffing. "Glad I caught you. And a pleasure to finally meet you, Mrs. Sanville!"

To her credit, she didn't gasp. The only thing that saved her was years of practice with four teasing brothers. Poker-faced, she returned the man's damp handshake, though every impulse inside her screamed to demand what he meant.

"I'm not Mrs. Sanville. If you want to see *Mr.* Sanville—"

"Ah, then it hasn't happened yet. All the better for me. I'll expect an invitation, of course."

Becca had the feeling any second he would slap her on the back with the same phony camaraderie that swelled his voice. Clearly the only cow this cowboy had ever tied into was a filet mignon.

But if a woman wanted information, she reckoned as how he'd warm up to a little flirtin'. "Guess I'll be needin' a name if I'm going to send an invitation, Mr....?"

"Griswold! Didn't Kody tell you? Call me Griz. You know, like the big bear?" His stomach shook when he laughed. "Now, just when *is* the date of your wedding, Miss . . . ?"

"Miss *Rebecca* to you, Griswold." J.S. erupted from the barn. He jerked a thumb over his shoulder. "Tully could use some help in the tack room, Miss Becca. I'll take care of Mr. Griswold."

Saved by the cook! She'd never seen J.S. so fired up. Mouthing "Thanks!" she sped by, tugging her hat low. Apparently J.S. didn't like Mr. Griswold, either. But the man had some kind of business here, or he wouldn't keep showing up. And why on earth would he think she and Kody were getting married?

Inside the barn, she slowed. Kody marry her? Nothing could be further from the truth. The only reason she was still here was because J.S. needed time to recuperate.

From the tack room, Tully's matter-of-fact voice rose and fell, explaining the equipment to the boys. He didn't sound as if he needed help.

Her help? Ranch hands didn't need help from the cook, especially one from Vermont! J.S. had sent her in to get rid of her! Whirling, she marched back out into the late afternoon sunlight.

J.S. stood where she'd left him, bowed legs apart, hands on hips, staring toward the ranch house where Mr. Griswold disappeared around the corner.

So J.S. had sent him packing. If she hadn't been so mad, she might have laughed.

"J.S.!" She charged ahead, only slightly mollified to see him cringe. Clearly he hadn't expected her to come back.

He raised his hands in defense. "Now, Miss Becca, don't you worry about—"

"What's going on, J.S.? Why does Mr. Griswold think Kody and I are getting married?"

"Listen, Miss Becca, Kody and Tom will be back any minute now, so if you want to help Kody..."

J.S.'s words faded, but like an echo, Callie's came rushing back. *I want to help, Kody... but not like this. I don't want the job.*

"J.S., what job did Callie turn down here at the ranch? And don't tell me it was to cook."

J.S. snatched off his hat and held it against his lean middle like a shield. "Miss Becca, I think we should be worrying about Tom right now and not—"

"If not for me, Kody might have hired that Coco Pelly woman. Would Griswold think Kody was marrying her?"

J.S.'s mouth fell open. His eyes widened. "Kokopelli woman? Where'd you hear *that?*"

"Callie told Kody to ask Coco Pelly about the job."

Amusement crept into his face as if someone were pouring it into him, softening his mouth into a smile, warming his dark eyes with delight.

"Damn it, J.S.—"

"Now, Miss Becca." He plunked his hat back onto his head and wrapped an arm around her shoulder. "Jest listen a minute." He began walking her toward the ranch house.

"There's an old Indian story 'bout a man who used to come through these here parts...with a bag of corn seed on his shoulder."

She tried to pull away. "J.S., save the stories for camp fire. I want answers."

"I'm fixin' to give 'em if you'll jest listen!" With surprising strength, he kept her moving. "The man stopped at every village to show the folks how to plant the seeds. Then when the moon was high and everyone was asleep, he walked through the cornfields and played his flute."

She scowled. "You'd better hurry."

J.S. just nodded. "An' when he played, the buds of the plant rose right up through the soil to follow his notes."

"And...?"

"That *man* is known as Kokopelli."

"Kokopelli?" She stared at him in confusion. "J.S., I don't understand how this—"

"Some say Kokopelli's music had such power that a woman would follow his songs and give herself right up to him."

Becca's breathing went shallow. Kody's music had drawn her, had called her out of the cabin, lured her through the silvery night. His songs had bewitched her until she'd given herself completely to the magic of his kiss. To a kiss she would never forget.

"The next mornin' the man was always gone. But the corn grew tall... an' the woman felt a fullness in her belly."

Kody had gone away, too. He'd drawn back into himself, and all she'd felt was a terrible emptiness in her heart.

At the back porch, she pulled free, fighting the urge to hug herself. "That's a nice story, J.S., but Kody hasn't planted corn and Callie told me he'd never marry, so don't—" The pounding of horses' hooves made her forget the rest of her protest. Kody galloped around the side of the ranch house and headed for the barn. He was leading the pinto. Its saddle was empty.

Her heart wrenched with fear. "Oh, J.S., no!" Breaking into a run, she reached the corral just as Kody dismounted to unlatch the gate.

Panic tightened her throat. "Where's Tom?"

Kody pushed the gate open and led the horses through. "I sent him back to the pueblo. A neighbor was headed that way in his truck."

She followed Kody through the corral, light-headed with relief. "Thank God you found him! Was he all right? Why didn't he come back with you?"

"He was scratched up some, but that'll heal. It's the hidden wounds that take time. He wasn't ready to deal with those." Kody sounded defensive... and defeated.

"Kody... I'm so sorry..."

He looked at her then. "It was my fault. I shouldn't have left you alone with them."

She could see the anguish in his eyes as clearly as if it mirrored her own. Disappointment. Heartache. Anger. She wanted to reach up and glide her palm along the hard plane of his cheek and brush away the darkness that deepened around his eyes. She wanted to tell him she finally understood, and she didn't care what mixture of blood flowed in his veins. A man was what he lived by and what he valued, not who his parents were.

She wanted to ask him for another chance with the boys.

"Kody..."

He bent to unfasten the saddle cinch.

Damn him, he was withdrawing again. "Mr. Griswold was here."

Kody mumbled a curse.

"He wants to know the date of the wedding." In the hovering silence, Becca thought her heart would stop.

Kody straightened. "There'll be no wedding." He jerked the saddle off. "And don't set a place for me at supper." Long strides carried him away toward the barn.

Kody was a man of few words, but he'd told her all she needed to know. She watched him disappear into the barn, knowing her job was about to come to an end.

Kody sat in the dim light of his room and stared at the sheet of paper on the scarred oak table that served as his desk. So Griswold had met Becca...and told her the terms of his father's will. He'd even had the gall to come into Kody's room to leave a note.

Hadn't the attorney gotten any of the messages Kody had spelled out so carefully to his secretary? Or had he just chosen to ignore them? Griswold struck him as the kind of scum bag who would enjoy stirring up trouble; and now the self-satisfied creep was going to foreclose on Kody's dream.

Kody shoved the paper away. Maybe he should just give up. What kind of dream was it, anyway, when he couldn't even reach a kid whose pain he understood too well? He had used every bit of his empathy to persuade Tom to come back and face the other boys, to learn to become proud of himself. But Tom had refused to even answer.

What kind of dream was it when he treated the woman who was trying to help him as if she were his pale-faced enemy?

Overhead he heard the muffled sound of boots moving across the polished wood floor. The bedsprings squeaked, followed by a thump...and then another. He imagined Becca gathering her boots up, setting them neatly inside the closet, then pulling out her suitcase and beginning to pack. The vision filled him with remorse... and something far more overwhelming.

Shoving up from the old Spanish table, he stalked to the window, yanked open the wood shutters and stared out at the night. The sky sparkled with stars—the same stars that had shone down on their kiss at the cabin. The memory brought a sharp oath.

What kind of a dream was it when he'd *used* Becca for his own ends... at the same time he was falling in love with her?

"Damn!" He doubled his fist and swung. Somehow he managed to stop before his knuckles smashed the shutter's wooden latilla slats. Whirling away from the window, he paced the length of the long room.

That's the way it had always been—the boiling Sanville passions checked by the patient peacefulness of his Hopi training. Denying him the release of anger... the cleansing forgetfulness of physical pain.

In spite of all his resolves, he'd fallen in love with Becca. There was no physical pain great enough to make him forget that. He'd have to live the rest of his life with the ache of wanting her, with the bittersweetness of remembering her—feeding sugar to his mules, bandaging a half-pint rebel, cheering a base run at the pueblo.

This morning at the pueblo, for the first time in his life, he'd actually imagined a child of his own, a dark-haired baby... with laughing silver-green eyes... and a dimple tucked into her cheek.

And with mixed blood.

How many times had he watched his mother hide her tears because her son's *bahana* blood kept him from being one with her people? How many times had he wanted to run away like Tom? He couldn't let that happen again.

Not to his child.

Not to Becca. Not to a Covington. The Covington blood bonds were too strong.

She didn't belong here, in a place where toddlers would never chase chickens in the yard and young sprouts would never rope calves for branding. Where there would be no family for a woman who was the very heart of one. He couldn't—he *wouldn't* ask her to suffer the life of an outsider.

Snatching the note from the table, he crushed it in his fist and flung it away. He *would not* repeat the sins of his father. Tomorrow morning he'd have Tully drive her to the airport. He wouldn't use her anymore...except as a memory locked in his heart.

Slouching back to the window, he stood staring out. Seeing nothing. Knowing in the morning Becca would already be packed and ready to go.

Suddenly he tensed. Breathed in deeply. A faint, delicate scent seemed to curl around him. A scent that could mean only one thing.

Chapter Eleven

Becca hesitated in the doorway, torn between conscience and wonder. Kody had made clear his room was
off-limits. But she had to talk to him.

He stood in front of the window, his broad back illu-
minated by a small desk lamp on the table behind him.
The light deepened the black of his ponytail and cast
shadows across the folds of his faded chambray shirt and
worn blue jeans.

Quickly she scanned his retreat—a room of heavy
beamed ceilings and soft leather furniture, bookshelves
overflowing with Indian pots and baskets and books of
all sizes. A place of earth tones and unstudied peacefulness.

Through the archway, she saw a whitewashed adobe
fireplace with his flute hanging on the side of the softly
rounded chimney. A fire reflected from the rough-hewn
posts of a bed.

It was the bed that forced her gaze back to him. How long had it been since she and Kody had struggled with mixing business and bedrooms? Once, the idea had tantalized. Now it just seemed impossible.

"You should be asleep."

His voice rode the air like the sonorous tones of a cello, making her inhale sharply. In spite of her sock-footed entry, he'd known she was there.

"I have to talk to you."

"There's nothing—"

"Yes there *is*." She'd come to the ranch to gain independence and self-reliance. It was time to prove that she'd learned them.

"Kody, I'm sorry about this afternoon...about Tom. I made some bad decisions. You have every right to be angry."

She paused. Gathered her courage. "I want to keep my job. I think I have a lot to offer The Journey. I want to talk to Tom. Maybe if a woman—"

"It wouldn't work. You don't have any concept of what it's like to be an outsider."

The harsh texture of his voice made her catch her breath. Maybe she didn't know, not like he did. Who could measure the intensity of another person's pain? She only knew she wanted to try to understand.

"Tell me what it's like."

The silence seemed to darken the shadows. Kody inhaled slowly, sending a shiver rippling up her neck. When he let his breath go, she could see the squareness of his shoulders give a little.

"Okay, Becca." Resignation deepened his voice. "Years ago, a white man... was inflamed by the dark beauty of an Indian woman. The man owned many beautiful things, and he wanted this woman, too.'' He hesitated, drew in a breath that sounded painful.

"So he courted her—in the way wealthy men do. Of course she fell in love with him.''

Kody was telling *his* story. The quiet detachment in his voice tugged at her heart, drawing her into the room.

"The woman was happy to marry him. She was even happier when he filled her with the seed that gave them a child. They had a boy... with skin the color of adobe. Then the man left.''

"He *left*?'' She felt the shocking words all the way to her heart.

"It's the custom of her people that the bride and groom live in the home of the bride's mother. He wouldn't do that.''

"But why didn't he take her *with* him?''

"It was the custom of *his* people that the bride and groom be of the same blood.''

This was what heartache felt like. How could Kody tell his story so passively? The urge to shake some kind of emotion from him pulled her farther into the room.

"But they didn't have to live with their families.'' In spite of herself, she moved still nearer. "Why didn't he bring her... to a place of their own?'' She'd almost said *here*.

"Because the man loved appearances more than people. He couldn't live with their differences. He decided he'd made a mistake.''

For the first time, she heard the anger in his voice, and she grew angry for him. The pain of being so totally rejected was almost more than she could comprehend.

"Your... The boy's mother must have been devastated.'' She could hardly bear to imagine what Kody's mother must have gone through.

"The Hopi are peaceful people. Sometimes too passive," he added quietly. "The woman accepted her fate. She knew the man didn't love her, not the way a man should love a wife. He hadn't given her the white buckskin moccasins a husband gives a Hopi bride."

Under the shielding cover of darkness, Kody was opening up. Would he let her reach out to comfort him? Gathering her courage, she moved around the large table, stopping just a few feet from him. "So the boy grew up feeling like an outsider."

At last he turned to face her. His gaze roiled with emotions.

Becca couldn't breathe. She had wanted to know his feelings, but she couldn't possibly have fathomed the depth of his wounds.

Kody's chin rose and his eyes hardened. "In his mother's pueblo, the boy had a home. But on his sixth birthday, his father took him away."

"I thought he didn't *want* him."

"He didn't. But the son wore the man's features...and his name. Appearances dictated that his son be raised—educated—accordingly." Kody spoke with icy correctness.

"His father sent him to boarding schools in the East. Summers he spent on wealthy cattle ranches...working. A much more *privileged* way of being an outsider." His voice rasped with harsh irony.

Becca's hand sought the golden knot at the dip of her throat. A child taken from his *mother,* forced to grow up without a home, without family to give protection and support, without siblings to tease and poke fun? Such rejection was beyond her understanding. Her heart ached with sympathy.

No wonder Kody had vowed not to repeat his father's mistake.

But Kody was wrong. His father's mistake wasn't in creating a half-breed child. It was not loving that child enough, not loving his wife enough to build a world of their own.

Now she understood the importance of his room. This was Kody's fortress, his refuge, a haven where he thought he could lock out hurt . . . and caring.

He thought he could lock her out.

She slid a step closer. "I think a boy like that would grow up very distrustful."

Kody didn't move, though his chin rose a fraction higher.

"I think when he became a man he would be afraid to care . . . for anyone."

A muscle in his jaw knotted, but still he didn't retreat.

Closing the gap between them, she searched his remote expression for some sign that he might relent.

"I think he would be too proud to ask a woman to love him." Reaching up, she touched his cheek, felt a shudder rack him. "Even if she did."

"Becca . . . ?"

His hand cupped her fingers against the smooth tautness of his cheek, held her there pressed tight as if he would never let her go. His eyes searched hers, dark with smoke, wide with wanting.

She waited, afraid to move. Afraid to speak and shatter this tremulous new desire that held them together so hesitantly.

In that moment, she knew that Allen had been wrong. Delinquent children wouldn't break her heart.

But Kody would. She'd fallen in love with him.

How could he send her away, Kody wondered, when she'd become more than he could possibly resist? So small without her boots, so exquisite even in jeans and a homely shirt. So desirable with her golden hair escaping from the scarf at her neck.

So loving.

Stifling a groan, Kody slid Becca's slender hand from his cheek to his mouth and pressed a kiss into the smooth softness of her palm. Drugged by her sweet, warm scent, he watched the anguish in her eyes shift and change, buffeting him with a rain of emotions he'd never dared dream of. Sympathy for the dark-skinned woman who'd been abandoned. Care and anguish for the lonely child who'd grown up without a home. Desire. For a man who'd become afraid to care.

No. Never afraid. He clasped her hand to his chest and lowered his mouth to hers.

At the touch of her soft lips, heat shot through him, embedding hot and wanting in his groin. Her mouth moved with his, reaching, seeking, molding to the devouring hunger of his kiss. He felt her rise to her toes, felt the lushness of her body arch against him as she slid her hands around his neck. Need and hunger spiraled through him and he pulled her closer, wanting to envelope her, to consume her, to make her his.

He kissed her eyes, her face, her ears, as if he could consume her. His hands wove into her hair, tugging the scarf free, letting silky strands flow through his fingers like liquid gold, enveloping him with the faint scent of shampoo.

Becca had dared to enter his fortress, and now she was breaching all his defenses. Like a sunflower blooming in cold shadows. Like hot springwater coiling through rocks. Like a shaft of warming sun that had found a chink in his walls and was filling his dark soul with life.

Beyond all reason, all caution, he found her lips again and deepened their kiss, sought to taste her sweetness. At his gentle probing, she opened, mixing her breath with his, welcoming him to the moist, warm softness of her mouth with an eager cry.

A heart song. Sweeter than the enchanting notes of a little yellow bird, her yearning sound called to him, sang to him, filled the lonely silence of his room. Overflowed the emptiness of his heart.

"Becca?" He whispered her name like a sacred word.

She leaned back to look deeply into his eyes. "Yes."

She answered the question he had no courage to ask. Scooping her into his arms, he held her gaze, saw in her eyes the joy, the wanting. Passions that matched his own.

Passions.

They almost won.

He almost broke every vow by which he'd chosen to live. But his conscience stirred, and his foot sent something skittering across the floor... like a dried leaf in a cold fall wind.

The sound tore him in two. He stood, raging with desire, watching himself agonize over a single, crumpled piece of paper—with the power to stay the Sanville passions. A paper that made sure he remembered what he was, that reminded him of what he had to do.

Carefully, gently, he lowered her to her feet.

"Kody...?"

Her anguished voice stabbed his long-guarded heart. He stepped back, knowing that what he was about to do was tantamount to tearing out a blade. Knowing he was about to die. "You shouldn't have come here, Becca."

"Kody, don't do this, please. I lo—"

"No!" He didn't want to hear what he saw in her eyes. He couldn't let her offer up her life. "I want you to leave. Tomorrow morning."

"But Kody, *why?* Doesn't this mean anything? Don't you feel any—"

"I've been using you, Becca. I needed a woman to fulfill the terms of my father's will. But they've been met, and J.S.'s niece is going to help with the cooking. I don't need you here anymore."

"Kody!"

He couldn't bear the pain in her eyes, the pleading in her voice. But it had to be this way. Like cutting off a limb... to save a life.

Becca would heal. Once she returned to the protective circle of her family, she would forget her cowgirl adventure. Her half-breed fantasies. The part of her heart she'd almost offered him.

With whatever will he had left, he forced himself to walk away from her. "You're fired, Becca." He stopped in the doorway of his room. "Tully will drive you to the airport in the morning."

Then he fled. Through the kitchen, out the back door, into the darkness. Wondering what kind of a life he could live... after she left with his heart.

Becca pressed a fist against her mouth, muffling the cry that strangled her throat and filled her eyes with tears. How could Kody do this after all he'd shared with her? The painful story of his life. His cherishing, hungering kisses.

Half-blinded, she found the padded arm of a high-backed chair and lowered herself into it. Too late, she realized it was probably his favorite, the place where he sat to do his paperwork or just to stare out the window—whenever he sought refuge in his fortress.

She could feel the warm imprint of his body, could smell his familiar scent mingled with the earthy flavor of the leather. In spite of herself, she leaned back, let the chair embrace her, give her whatever solace it had to offer.

How could Kody have fired her? His kiss had been as fierce and wanting as hers. He must have felt something for her. No man could kiss like that without feeling more than heat.

Damn it, she didn't believe he didn't care about her. Care *for* her. She *wouldn't* believe it.

Straightening, she whisked the moisture from her lashes and blew into a tissue. She'd simply refuse to believe him. She'd decline the opportunity to leave. Somehow she had to convince him to keep her at the Sanville Star as a part of The Journey. As a part of his life.

On her feet now, she stooped to retrieve her scarf where Kody had let it slide to the floor. It lay near a crumpled piece of white paper.

Stuffing the scarf into her pocket, she picked up the paper and carried it back to the table, unable to stop herself from glancing at the pinched, back-slanted handwriting that crawled in and out of the crinkles. All she could make out were the letters *Grisw.*

Griswold. A message from the man who'd been there that afternoon. A message that was none of her business, she reminded herself. Reluctantly, she laid the wadded paper on the table.

Griswold had called her Mrs. Sanville. For some reason, he'd thought she had married Kody. Didn't that make his message her business, too?

With fingertips, she retrieved the ball of paper and held it by the edges, feeling terribly guilty. But not guilty enough. Slowly she unfolded the creases and wrinkles until the words lay in straight lines across its creased surface. They were upside-down.

She could still stop, still save herself from committing this invasion.

No, she couldn't. Quickly she turned the page right side up and read.

Kody,
Met Miss Rebecca. Quite a catch . . . if this woman really *is* going to marry you. I'll be back tomorrow at 10:00 for proof. Otherwise, I'll start proceedings to sell. Remember the terms—no wife, no heir, no ranch.

                                        Griswold

Heart pounding, Becca read the message again. With every sentence, the fragile hopes she'd clung to splintered and fell away.

What had Kody said—that he'd been using her to fulfill the terms of his father's will? With the words staring her in the face, she couldn't refuse to believe him anymore.

I want to help you, Kody, but not like this. Now she understood Callie's refusal. Callie wouldn't pretend to be his wife.

You must ask Kokopelli, she'd said. Right. Just put in a little bid to the musical god of fertility and lure Kody some other woman. Preferably a nice, gullible one.

Then Becca had marched right over and offered herself up on the proverbial silver platter.

She crushed the paper in her fist, let it fall back to the floor. Even when she'd shown up like an answer to his prayers, Kody hadn't wanted her at the ranch. Not a tenderfoot, a greenhorn *debutante* from the city. But he'd hired her anyhow... because he needed a fiancée, a bride-to-be. A *front*.

Fighting back tears, Becca dashed from the room and through the moonlit kitchen. Kody hadn't even thought enough of her to ask her to *play* the part. He'd kept the charade from her the whole time. He'd *lied* to her... because he didn't think she could handle it.

Just like her family.

Grasping the golden knot at her throat, Becca stumbled through the darkened ranch house and up the stairs. Inside her room, she closed the door and leaned against it, her eyes squeezed closed. Warm moisture tracked down her cheeks.

When her heartbeat finally slowed, she straightened and swept the tears from her face.

Moving through the darkness, she went to the closet and pulled out her suitcase.

Chapter Twelve

Ask Kokopelli.

Becca dropped her suitcase on the bed and stood in the darkness of her bedroom, wondering why Callie's words still whispered in her head when her heart was slowly breaking.

Ask Kokopelli. Abandoning the suitcase, she moved to the open window and gazed out at the yard below. It loomed with shadows in the faint light of the rising moon—Kody's thunder moon, gone gibbous and lopsided since their fateful trip to the cabin.

Nearby, a cricket played its one-note love song, but though she strained to hear the spiraling melody of a flute, wind-stirred leaves were all that rustled through the air. The sounds mingled with the sad ache in her chest and sent a shiver skimming across her shoulders.

Kody was out there somewhere. If only she could go to him, talk to him. But she knew he wouldn't listen. He'd learned too young not to trust, to build fortresses around his feelings. Too bad she'd never learned the same.

It was all she could do to turn her back on the lonely night sounds. But there was no haunting music out there for her, no mythical being to intervene on her behalf. Kokopelli was a myth. So were the feelings she'd thought Kody felt for her. He might feel desire, but he didn't love her.

It was time for her to grow up. Time to prove she'd learned self-reliance. She lit the small night lamp on the dresser and pulled the scarf from her pocket. Gathering her hair behind her neck, she tied it back tightly, refusing to remember what Kody's touch had done to her when he'd set it free. Opening a drawer, she lifted out a handful of lacy underwear and padded reluctantly to the bed.

She wasn't needed here anymore. That's what Kody had said. With J.S.'s niece helping in the kitchen and the terms of the will fulfilled—

Becca stopped. *"No wife, no heir, no ranch."* That's what Griswold's note had said. Had Kody found another woman to play his wife? She dropped onto the bed, clutching the lacy scraps of clothing to her chest and struggling with deepening sadness.

Had Kody decided he wanted the ranch badly enough to marry? If that were true, Callie would be his most obvious choice—the woman who clearly had loved him for a long time. The woman who yearned to give him children.

In spite of growing hopelessness, Becca made herself keep working. She dumped her underwear into the case and crossed to the walk-in closet. Inside, she jammed a row of hangers together and hoisted them off the rack.

Callie could give Kody children with skin the color of copper. Children with less mixed blood.

The realization left her standing in the middle of the room hugging the bundle of clothes. Fumbling for a sleeve, she managed to catch the tears before they overflowed.

Damn. She had to stop this. Crying didn't change anything.

At the bed, she threw down the clothes and wiped her eyes. The effort didn't make her feel any better, but at least she could see to pack. She'd get everything together tonight so she could leave early in the morning. Right after breakfast... when everyone had gone off to work.

Her departure would be a lot different from Tom's. Thoughts of the defiant youngster stopped her in the middle of folding a shirt. The boy's refusal to return had disturbed Kody badly. Was he still planning to take the other boys on The Journey?

Becca stared at the window, filled only with reflections of the room. What did a man do when his dreams clashed with his vows? Would Kody marry Callie? Or would he give it all up—the ranch, The Journey, the chance to help kids—because of his father's failings?

Had Kody decided to give up his dream?

Leaving her shirt half-folded in the suitcase, she searched for her jewelry bag in the nightstand drawer. Allen's ring still lay in the center pocket where she'd put it the night before she came to the Sanville Star. She could feel its hard shape through the soft velvet.

What did a *woman* do when her dreams clashed with what was expected of her? Was she any better than Kody, letting him send her back to her overprotective family, to comfortable, attentive Allen?

Reluctantly, she slipped the ring out and watched light dance from the facets of the two-carat marquise diamond. Its brilliance reminded her of starlight. Not a good idea to think of starlight.

She spread the fingers of her left hand and marveled at how tan she'd become. The pale line on her ring finger had completely disappeared. Fighting a mixture of resistance and guilt, she slipped the ring into place. The time had come to put it back on.

The diamond looked big and conspicuous on her hand—a hand too dry and sunburned to be feminine, with unpainted nails cut too short for a wedding. But she liked the way her hands looked now. Strong and capable. Like working hands. Like the hands of a rancher.

For a long time, she stood in the middle of the dimly lit room staring at her hand. Thinking.

At last she moved. Returning to the bed, she finished packing, her movements deliberate and efficient now. She set the suitcase outside the door, keeping her backpack for last-minute items in the morning, along with her best jeans, ruffled denim shirt, boots and hat. They would do. Nobody dressed for airplane flights anymore.

She switched off the light, slipped into her nightgown and padded to the window. Outside, a million million stars glittered back at her.

Ask Kokopelli, Callie had said. Becca hugged herself to ward off the cool breeze . . . and to give herself courage. From the depths of her heart, she sent up a silent appeal for understanding, willing it to fly, on the notes of Kokopelli's flute, to wherever Allen was tonight. Then she climbed into the bed.

Under the lightweight cover, she gave the ring a twist and told herself to go to sleep. She knew now what she had to do.

"I can't find Miss Becca, boss."

"You *what?*" Kody stopped buffing his caramel-colored saddle and stared up at Tully. The man stood in the tack room entrance, head down, watching his booted foot push straw back and forth on the barn floor.

"She disappeared after breakfast. I got her stuff from the upstairs hall and I checked everywhere in the house, but there's no sign of her."

Frowning, Kody straightened and pressed a sleeve against the sweat at his temples. He tried to quell his growing agitation. Even after no sleep, he'd rather be chopping the hell out of a bunch of logs than cleaning his saddle. But he needed to look halfway respectable when Griswold arrived.

"Where's J.S.? He'll know where she is." Kody didn't even try to temper his anger. J.S. had made sure breakfast was more of an ordeal than a man could stand.

If Kody had thought for a minute Becca was going to be there, he'd have fled the house long before sunup. But there she'd been, moving around the kitchen in that frilly denim blouse and those body-hugging jeans, claiming J.S. wasn't feeling up to cooking.

She'd acted as if nothing had happened last night. As if Kody hadn't fired her. As if he hadn't kissed her. As if he hadn't come that close to taking her to his bed. And the whole time, she'd looked more beautiful, more tempting, than she had her first day here.

She'd looked different. Her hair was all loose and curly, like a halo of spun gold lighting her face...the way she'd worn it at Trey's wedding. Kody had wanted to touch her, to scoop his hands through her hair as he had last night. He'd wanted to kiss her breathless right there in the kitchen.

"Can't find J.S., either, boss."

Kody snapped the chamois hard. "What do you mean you can't find J.S.? You've got to find him." He glared at Tully, the task of saddle cleaning all but forgotten. "I want Becca out of here before Griswold arrives."

Becca had been too quiet this morning. Too composed. Not like the bubbling bundle of energy who'd livened up the house ever since her arrival. Not the frothy East Coast debutante, either. In such a short time, he'd watched her become a capable ranch hand, a self-reliant woman.

Or was it simply that his perceptions had changed? All he knew was that when she'd poured his coffee and smiled at him this morning, he'd wanted her to stay.

Which was exactly why he'd escaped to the barn—to get away from the domestic scents of pancakes and brewed coffee . . . and her own delicate fragrance. From those silver-green eyes full of warmth and acceptance. Full of questions.

"Boss?"

"*What?*"

"Griswold drove up a minute ago."

Kody finally let loose with the oath he'd been stifling since breakfast, a resounding *bahana* curse that gave him no satisfaction at all. Only reminded him of his father.

He flung the chamois down. "Go see if J.S. has her holed up in the bunkhouse. Then get her to the airport. I don't want her fending off that two-bit attorney again."

Tully squinted at Kody. "Boss, you sure—?"

"Yes! I'm sure!" he shouted. "Now, *go.*"

"Right." The corners of Tully's mouth twisted downward as he pivoted toward the far door of the barn.

Kody swallowed another oath. He didn't need ranch hands telling him who he should keep on the payroll. Grabbing his hat, he slammed it onto his head and stretched his legs toward the front of the ranch house, trying to outdistance his anger.

He didn't need J.S.'s brand of after-breakfast wisdom, either. *You send that woman away and you'll jest prove you're so dumb you couldn't teach a hen to cluck.* In all their time together, Kody had never heard J.S. shout. Remembering Tully's look of disgust, Kody added guilt to the herd of feelings that dogged him. *He'd* never shouted before, either.

Maybe J.S. was right. Maybe he *was* just plain obtuse. Couldn't convince an eleven-year-old kid to come play cowboy. Couldn't school his own heart to stop falling in love with Becca.

But he couldn't involve her in his problems anymore. If he hurried, he'd catch Griswold in front of the house. It wouldn't take much to set the shyster straight. Then he'd run him off.

After that, he'd saddle his horse and head out to where the kids were learning to mend fences. He wouldn't say goodbye. He meant never to see Becca again.

Rounding the corner of the house, Kody saw the suit-clad attorney climbing the front steps. Halfway up, the man stopped to fiddle with a bright yellow flower in his lapel.

Kody's anger flared all over again. Griswold must have picked a marigold from the flowers Becca had planted in front of the house. He damn well better not have done any damage.

"Hey, Griswold!"

"Kody! You're a hard man to find." He continued to fuss with the flower.

Swallowing a scathing response, Kody roared toward the stairs. "Did you get my messages?"

Just then, the screen door swung open, and Becca strode across the porch. "Mr. Griswold! How nice to see you again."

Kody nearly stumbled. *"Becca—!"*

"Why, Miss Rebecca, what a pleasant surprise. I didn't expect to find you here."

Griswold's smirk reminded Kody of a snake. His hands ached for a snake-whacking shovel.

"Why, where else would I *be,* Mr. Griswold?" Becca flashed the attorney a dazzling smile, then turned one of equal magnitude on Kody. "Kody, you're just in time."

His response came out close to a growl.

Becca wrapped Griswold's arm through hers. "I've got fresh coffee and muffins *right* out of the oven. Come on in while I tell you how Kody taught me to make ranch coffee." She led Griswold into the ranch house, sending Kody a tantalizing glance over her shoulder.

He'd kill Griswold, that was all...right after he locked Becca in a closet. Stomping up the porch stairs, he followed them into the house, slamming the screen door behind him.

"Becca!" Kody charged into the dining room.

Her hand didn't even waver while she filled Griswold's mug, but her face softened into a smile. She couldn't have looked any more enticing if she'd tried. Kody felt his anger begin to deflate.

"Kody, you are *such* a bear till you've had your second cup of coffee. Let's get you tamed a little before we talk business. Come sit down, sweetheart."

He stopped stone still and stared at her. *Sweetheart?*
"Becca, you need to—"

"No, I didn't forget." With a smile that was both patient and mischievous, she pulled out his chair, then marched over to him. "Cream and sugar, right on the table. And your favorite banana muffins."

The shock of her hands on his arm blanked his mind of anything but her touch. Before he could even think to resist, she nudged him to the chair and almost hip-checked him into it.

"He's such a hard worker, Mr. Griswold, I can hardly get him to sit two minutes." She stood behind Kody, hands on his shoulders—holding him firmly down.

Awareness raced across his back and radiated up his neck. He couldn't have moved if he'd sat on a cactus. She inched her hands down his chest on either side, enveloping him in a wave of heat . . . and panic.

"But I shouldn't complain," she murmured somewhere in the vicinity of his ear.

Her hair brushed the side of his face just as her fragrance engulfed him. Like a drowning man, he tried not to breathe, tried to struggle, but her faint breath sent tremors shuddering through him.

"After all, we're so anxious for the ranch to be in good shape. For the wedding and all."

Wedding! The word should have brought him roaring up out of the chair, but that was the precise moment she chose to brush her lips against his cheek.

Magic. Sorcery. He could feel it—a kiss so soft and gentle it might be the kiss of a woman in love. She'd done it on purpose, he was sure, but that didn't lessen the shock. His whole body felt paralyzed. Well, almost. Any more of this, and he wouldn't be able to get up from the table for half a week.

"Becca..." he pleaded, rasping the hoarseness from his throat.

"Here, sweetheart, drink some coffee and clear that dust out." Reaching around him, she pulled his cup nearer.

Kody almost choked—because her lush body pressed against his back. Because on her hand she wore an enormous diamond ring. Because he caught sight of her smile, and she was enjoying every single second of his misery.

Grabbing his mug, he downed half the contents, glad for the burn, wishing it were something stronger. What in the devil was Becca doing? Did she honestly think Griswold would believe *Kody* gave her that ring?

"Well, well, *well*." Griswold reached for a muffin and began peeling the paper away. "Looks like you two must have mended your little spat."

"Yes, and we've been so busy, Mr. Griswold, but I was glad when Kody told me you were coming out this morning. Wasn't I, sweetheart?" Becca straightened slowly, blowing a gentle puff into his ear.

Hen flesh raced all the way down his arm. Kody wanted to wring her neck—right after he got done kissing her.

"We wanted you to know—" Becca ignored Kody's tension "—you *will* be getting an invitation to the wedding. It'll be in September." Her hands squeezed Kody's shoulders.

She might as well have kicked him in the behind. "Uh, yeah," he added. "We're taking the cattle to summer pasture first, and we've got these boys to look after."

Becca's hands patted his shoulders gently, and Kody wondered if Griswold recognized her subtle applause.

Without missing a beat, she leaned around Kody's shoulder and cast him a sideways glance. Her eyes were full of laughter. "We're giving you fair warning, Mr. Griswold. You're invited to the shower, too, soon as our first little one's on the way. We'll expect a real nice gift."

This time Kody did choke.

"Don't drink your coffee so fast, darlin'." Leaning back, she thumped him solidly on the back. "Now, Mr. Griswold, what do we have to sign to be sure our baby will be making the Sanville Star his home?"

"You don't have to sign anything, Miss Rebecca, but I'm real glad I came out this morning." He reached for another muffin. "I was going to start the search for buyers, but looks like that won't be necessary." Stacking the muffin paper on top of the two already on his plate, he cut himself another pat of butter. "You *do* make wonderful muffins, Miss Rebecca.

"Where was I? Oh, yes, the trust doesn't end till next June, but I 'spect there'll be a new little Sanville on the way by then. All's I'll need are copies of the marriage and birth certificates." He gave Kody an exaggerated wink. "Old Reynard Sanville sure arranged for a mighty fine present."

Kody wanted to bust the man right in the mouth. To his relief, Becca stepped between them. "Another cup of coffee, Mr. Griswold? How about another muffin?"

"Well, thank you, I do believe I—"

Enough was enough! Kody shot up, shoving his chair backward, glowering at Griswold.

"I do believe I'll just be on my way." Griswold stood almost as abruptly, fingertips on the tabletop.

"Good." Kody shoved the bench back to let the lawyer out. "I'll walk you to your car."

Becca had done her good deed. Now all Kody wanted was to get out of here before he started taking her seriously. He moved toward the door, but Becca got in his way.

"Thanks for coming in, sweetheart." Resting her hands on his shirtfront, she reached up to kiss him softly on the mouth. Just as quickly, she turned toward Griswold.

Well, hell.

Catching her by the hand, he swung her back into his arms, felt the lush softness of her body close with his, heard her surprised intake of breath. It sent a shaft of sweet desire licking through him.

Then he was kissing her, awed by the perfection of her lips, amazed at her fleeing resistance. She leaned into his embrace, and her arms encircled his neck. He could feel the smile on her lips.

A bittersweet sigh warmed his cheek, a sound that hurt him to hear. The next moment she was gone, taking Griswold out the front door, reciting the ingredients for camp-fire coffee as she went.

Kody stood rooted to the floor. Becca knew about the will. She knew he'd been using her, yet she'd stepped in to save the Sanville Star for him. Could she possibly feel for him what he—?

No. Don't be a damn fool, he told himself. Becca was the golden flower at the heart of a lily-white family. Her suitcase was on the front porch waiting to see her home to them. She could never give her heart to a bronze-skinned man. He would never ask her. He loved her too much to invite her into the life of an outsider.

She was simply a gracious and generous Covington. Even after he'd treated her so badly, she was trying to give him back his dreams. But what would happen to his dreams when Griswold learned she'd gone?

Did Kody even care anymore...if Becca wasn't here to share them?

"Kody?" The screen door slapped shut behind Becca, and she hurried to the dining room, stopping under the archway. Coffee mugs still dotted the table, along with a plate half-full of muffins. There was no sign of Kody.

All the hopes that had fluttered up when he'd kissed her struggled to stay airborne. How could he have gotten away so quickly?

"Kody, I have good news." She hurried into the kitchen, came to an unsure stop at the sight of his closed door. But her hesitation didn't last. She would not let her hopes plummet. She would find him. Marching across the room, she knocked loudly.

"Kody, I have something to tell you." The door wasn't latched. She pushed it open. The top of the ornate oak table lay bare, and the whole room looked much too tidy. Felt too empty.

Dashing through the kitchen, she rushed outside. She hadn't heard the truck drive away from the front of the house, but Kody might have escaped on horseback. Her heart raced ahead of her feet.

"Kody?" She called into the barn, and the sound echoed back at her from the empty stalls, sending a pair of doves chirping their frightened complaints.

Becca felt the emptiness here, too. Kody wasn't inside and neither was his horse. The message was clear.

What if he'd gone to the cabin?

She'd just have to follow, that was all, because she was not giving up now. Marching back into the sunlight, she headed toward the corral to get a horse.

Thwack.

The muted sound slowed her steps. The second blow kicked her into a run, her feet barely touching the ground all the way to the edge of the clearing.

He stood in the middle, bare to his waist, sweat gleaming on his copper torso, his dark hair tied behind his neck. He was so beautiful. And so damned stubborn.

She watched him swing the ax into a high arc, saw the muscles of his torso knot and stretch as he drove the blade deep into the log in front of him. Scowling, he bent to work it free.

"Kody?"

He tensed but didn't look up, just kept worrying the ax blade.

She took a few steps into the clearing, her determination wavering. "I have good news. Callie called after breakfast. She said Tom wants to come back for The Journey. I told her to bring him over this afternoon."

He worked the blade free, but some of the fierceness seemed to have gone out of him. Not much to hang her hopes on, but she wouldn't give up yet.

Resting the ax on the log, he prepared for another swing. "You should have asked me. You don't work here anymore."

He might as well have put her heart on the block, his words cut so deep. "Damn it, Kody, you can't fire me. There's too much to do around here. You need my help."

The ax paused in midair, then dropped to his side.

"Besides...we have to make wedding plans," she finished feebly.

He straightened to his full height, shoulders back, head high, and stood like a bronze statue, aloof and indomitable.

"I won't marry you, Becca."

"Why?" Her voice only trembled a little.

"You wear another man's ring."

Her eyes flew to the engagement ring she'd forgotten to take off. Stretching her fingers, she removed it quickly and buried it in her pocket, all the time aware of Kody's gaze.

"I've known Allen since we were in kindergarten. He's always been there . . . like another brother. I thought I loved him, but, Kody, it was never like—"

Muttering a word she'd never heard, he stooped and gathered the clutter of split logs into his arms. "There's nothing here for you, Becca. Go back to your family."

She couldn't let him withdraw from her the way he always had before. "Kody, do you love me?"

His head shot up, and some of the logs tumbled from his arms. His gaze locked with hers, dark and searching.

She stepped nearer. "Tell me you don't love me and I'll leave."

Disbelief and pain struggled in his eyes. "No." Rising, he stalked to the woodpile.

Her heart all but stopped. He'd turned away, but he hadn't said he didn't love her. She had to hold on to that.

Following him, she stood near the woodpile and watched him stack the logs. "I asked for this job because everyone in my family always told me how to run my life."

She crossed her arms to shore up her determination. "I've had men telling me what to do and making my decisions since I was a kid. It's time *I* decide how I want to live. And *where* I want to live."

Kody carried another log to the chopping block and balanced it in place.

"Kody, I want to live with you."

He drove the ax into the log—hard. "No." He jerked the ax free. "I won't use you anymore."

"You'd give up the ranch and all your dreams just to prove you won't use me?" In the stark silence that followed, Becca held her breath and prayed.

Slowly Kody turned. He squared his shoulders and met her gaze. His eyes were ravaged with anguish. "Yes." The single word resonated in the silence like the final stroke on a cello.

Becca exhaled slowly, feeling the last of her doubts give way. Kody wouldn't marry her to keep the ranch.

Smiling with brave new hope, she stepped in front of him. "I'm still offering to marry you," she murmured.

He searched her face, and that dear V settled between his eyes. She wanted to reach up and smooth it away.

"We're too different. We come from different worlds." He tried to move around her. "I won't repeat my father's mistakes."

Sidestepping, she planted herself once more in his path. "Differences don't cause pain, Kody. It's not being loved that does." She gazed up at him, imploring him not to go.

"You're not like your father. You wouldn't abandon your wife or your son. You'd make a home for them, a place of love. A place to belong. This place."

He didn't move, but she could see the struggle working behind his eyes, the uncertainty of giving up old beliefs, the risks of accepting what she said.

"I love you, Kody." She touched the golden knot at her throat and knew she'd finally learned to do what was right for her, no matter what the risks.

She'd also learned bullheaded single-mindedness. Closing the gap between them, she planted a finger smack in the middle of his sleek chest.

"Tell me you don't love me, and I'll get out of your life." She braced for his rejection, praying he couldn't feel her quaking heartbeat through her fingertip. She watched him wrestle with his feelings until she couldn't bear the silence any longer.

"Otherwise, I'd appreciate if you'd stop making decisions for me and our future children, and pick out a wedding date instead."

She was prepared to see him glower. She knew he might refuse to answer, might even walk away. But one dark brow rose slowly and then the other. In sheer breathlessness, she watched that wonderful, elusive humor creep into his eyes.

"How about sometime in September?"

"Kody!" She launched herself into his arms.

He welcomed her with an open heart, holding her so tight she knew he'd never let her go. His mouth closed over hers, and he kissed her until she had to pull away, laughing and gasping for air. Nibbling her lower lip gently, he set her feet back on the ground and rested his hands at her waist.

"I love you, Becca. But you must be sure. It won't be what you've lived before. Some people won't accept. Your family may not—"

She touched her fingers to his lips. "I'm sure."

For a long time he searched her eyes, his face drawn with seriousness. Slowly a smile threatened the corners of his mouth. He leaned to her ear.

"I can't choose a wedding date," he whispered, sending delicious shivers up and down her neck.

She tugged back to look up at him. *"Why?"*

"First I have to learn to make a pair of white buck-skin moccasins." Promises filled his eyes and his smile broadened, tracing lines in his face...wonderful new lines of happiness.

"I can wait."

She could wait for the Hopi gift from a husband to his bride. She could wait for the promise of a fullness in her belly. She could wait for a lifetime of belonging to each other.

"But not very long." Smiling, she reached up to kiss him again.

And from somewhere not too far away, she heard the silver-dusted notes of Kokopelli's flute.

* * * * *

FORTUNE'S Children™

Bestselling Author

LINDA
TURNER

Continues the twelve-book series—FORTUNE'S CHILDREN—
in November 1996 with Book Five

THE WOLF AND THE DOVE

Adventurous pilot Rachel Fortune and traditional Native American
doctor Luke Greywolf set sparks off each other the minute they met.
But widower Luke was tormented by guilt and vowed never to love
again. Could tempting Rachel heal Luke's wounded heart so they
could share a future of happily ever after?

MEET THE FORTUNES—a family whose legacy is greater than riches.
Because where there's a will...there's a *wedding!*

*A CASTING CALL TO
ALL FORTUNE'S CHILDREN FANS!*
If you are truly fortunate,
you may win a trip to
Los Angeles to audition for
Wheel of Fortune®. Look for
details in all retail Fortune's Children titles!

WHEEL OF FORTUNE is a registered trademark of Califon Productions, Inc.©
1996 Califon Productions, Inc. All Rights Reserved.

Look us up on-line at: http://www.romance.net

FC-5-C

MILLION DOLLAR SWEEPSTAKES

SWP-M96

As seen on TV!
Free Gift Offer

With a Free Gift proof-of-purchase from any Silhouette® book,
you can receive a beautiful cubic zirconia pendant.

This gorgeous marquise-shaped stone is a genuine cubic
zirconia—accented by an 18" gold tone necklace.

(Approximate retail value $19.95)

Send for yours today...
compliments of *Silhouette*®

To receive your free gift, a cubic zirconia pendant, send us one original proof-of-purchase, photocopies not accepted, from the back of any Silhouette Romance™, Silhouette Desire®, Silhouette Special Edition®, Silhouette Intimate Moments® or Silhouette Yours Truly™ title available in August, September, October, November and December at your favorite retail outlet, together with the Free Gift Certificate, plus a check or money order for $1.65 U.S./$2.15 CAN. (do not send cash) to cover postage and handling, payable to Silhouette Free Gift Offer. We will send you the specified gift. Allow 6 to 8 weeks for delivery. Offer good until December 31, 1996 or while quantities last. Offer valid in the U.S. and Canada only.

Free Gift Certificate

Name: _____

Address: _____

City: _____ State/Province: _____ Zip/Postal Code: _____

Mail this certificate, one proof-of-purchase and a check or money order for postage and handling to: SILHOUETTE FREE GIFT OFFER 1996. In the U.S.: 3010 Walden Avenue, P.O. Box 9077, Buffalo NY 14269-9077. In Canada: P.O. Box 613, Fort Erie, Ontario L2Z 5X3.

FREE GIFT OFFER   084-KMD
ONE PROOF-OF-PURCHASE
To collect your fabulous FREE GIFT, a cubic zirconia pendant, you must include this
original proof-of-purchase for each gift with the properly completed Free Gift Certificate.

084-KMD-R

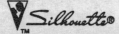

Add a double dash of romance to your
festivities this holiday season
with two great stories in

*Christmas
Celebration*

Featuring full-length stories by bestselling authors

Kasey Michaels
Anne McAllister

These heartwarming stories of love triumphing
against the odds are sure to add some extra
Christmas cheer to your holiday season. And this
distinctive collection features **two full-length novels,**
making it the perfect gift at great value—for
yourself or a friend!

Available this December at your favorite retail outlet.

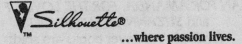

...where passion lives.

XMASCEL

The collection of the year!
NEW YORK TIMES BESTSELLING AUTHORS

Linda Lael Miller
Wild About Harry

Janet Dailey
Sweet Promise

Elizabeth Lowell
Reckless Love

Penny Jordan
Love's Choices

and featuring
Nora Roberts
The Calhoun Women

This special trade-size edition features four of the wildly
popular titles in the Calhoun miniseries together in
one volume—a true collector's item!

Pick up these great authors and a chance to win
a weekend for two in New York City at the
Marriott Marquis Hotel on Broadway! We'll pay
for your flight, your hotel—even a Broadway show!

Available in December at your favorite retail outlet.

NEW YORK

Marriott.
MARQUIS

HARLEQUIN® ♥ Silhouette®

NYT1296-R

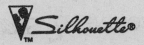